Elements of

# Hindustani Classical Music

# New Vistas in Indian Performing Arts

1. **Hindustānī Music and the Aesthetic Concept of Form**; by Anjali Mittal (ISBN 978-81-246-0134-1)
2. **Hindustani Sangeet and a Philosopher of Art** — Music, Rhythm and Kathak Dance *vis-à-vis* Aesthetics of Susanne K. Langer; by S.K. Saxena (ISBN 978-81-246-0180-8)
3. **Speaking of Dance** — The Indian Critique; by Mandakranta Bose (ISBN 978-81-246-0172-3)
4. **Performing Artistes in Ancient India**; by Iravati (ISBN 978-81-246-0207-2)
5. **Ritual as Ideology** : Text and Context in Teyyam; by T.V. Chandran (ISBN 978-81-246-0275-1)
6. **Tantra-Mantra-Yantra in Dance** : An Exposition of Kathaka; by Ranjana Srivastava (ISBN 978-81-246-0268-3)
7. **Hindustani Music** : A Tradition in Transition; by Deepak Raja (ISBN 978-81-246-0320-8)
8. **The Art of Tabalā Rhythm** — Essential, Tradition and Creativity; by Sudhir Kumar Saxena (ISBN 978-81-246-0368-0)
9. **Kathaka, The Tradition**— Fusion and Diffusion; by Ranjana Srivastava (ISBN 978-81-246-0473-1)
10. **Elements of Hindustani Classical Music**; by Shruti Jauhari (ISBN 978-81-246-0568-4)
11. **Khayāla Vocalism**: Continuity within Change; by Deepak Raja (ISBN 978-81-246-0481-6)
12. **The Rāga-ness of Rāgas** : Rāgas Beyond the Grammar; by Deepak Raja (ISBN 978-81-246-0835-7)
13. **The Royal Temple Theatre of Krishnattam**; by Martha Bush Ashton-Sikora (ISBN 978-81-246-0836-4)

New Vistas in Indian Performing Arts, no. 10

# Elements of Hindustani Classical Music

Shruti Jauhari

*with a foreword by*
K.J. Yesudas

DK PRINTWORLD
Publishers of Indian Traditions

Cataloging in Publication Data — DK
[Courtesy: D.K. Agencies (P) Ltd. <docinfo@dkagencies.com>]

**Jauhari, Shruti, 1969- author.**
Elements of Hindustani classical music / Shruti Jauhari; with a foreword by K.J. Yesudas.
pages cm. – (New vistas in Indian performing arts; no. 10)
"First published in India, 2011, Second revised edition, 2015" – Title page verso.
Includes bibliographical references and index.
ISBN 9788124607992 (Hb)

1. Hindustani music – History and criticism. I. Title. II. Series: New vistas in Indian performing arts ; no. 10.

LCC ML338.J38 2020 | DDC 780.954 23


First published in India, 2011
Second revised edition, 2015
Reprinted in 2020, 2026
ISBN 13: 978-81-246-0799-2 (HB)
ISBN 13: 978-81-246-0800-5 (PB)



*Printed and Published by*:
D.K. Printworld (P) Ltd.
*Regd. Office*: '*Vedasri*', F-395, Sudarshan Park
(Metro Station: ESI Hospital), New Delhi - 110 015
*Phones*: (011) 4172 2626, 9871394815
*e-mail*: indology@dkprintworld.com
*Web*: www.dkprintworld.com

To
My Parents
Mrs. Geeta Verma and Dr. R.M. Verma

# Foreword

IT is my parents who have influenced me to observe that music is universal and has no religion. The way we present and render any kind of music results in various styles and forms such as Arabic, Chinese, Carnatic, etc. However, the notation remains the same. Hence I believe that music is one, like *Param Brahma.*

Great scholars and musicians from our rich cultural heritage have paved the path of knowledge and it is our duty to seek, acquire and share this knowledge further.

Shruti, who is like my child, has made an effort in a small way through this book which is aimed at providing the basic knowledge of Hindustani classical music for the beginners and curious *rasikas*.

I have gone through the contents of this book and find that it would be extremely useful to those interested in learning and understanding the basic nuances and details of Hindustani classical music.

The first chapter deals with the history and evolution of Hindustani music in a comprehensive manner. I believe that it is important to know the history of any art form before pursuing it further. The second and third chapters are very informative as they deal with all the basic terms such as: *Rāg, Tāl, Khayāl Gāyakī, Tān*s and so on. These are the terms which not only a student of music seeks to understand, but also a *rasika* who is a regular audience of concerts in the present times. Although the very concept of *gharānā*, or specialized music schools, is diminishing in this electronic age, it is still important that a student has a composite knowledge about them. The chapter on *gharānā*s and the eminent musicians (along with their photographs) would prove useful and perhaps even motivating in the journey of music learning. The chapter on various instruments would be extremely relevant as it is often not given its due by the voice of students. The last chapter on various *Rāg*s and their details has been incorporated as a ready reference to the students as well as to the connoisseurs.

Thus the book broadly covers all the important and relevant topics in a compact manner for complete understanding of Hindustani classical music. The language used is also simple, spoken English for a clear understanding of the subject.

I hope that this book will be beneficial to all those who wish to learn, acquire knowledge and appreciate the beautiful Hindustani classical form of music.

*October, 2010* **K.J. Yesudas**

# Preface

IT IS rightly said that music has no language and quality music, be it Western, Carnatic or Hindustani, appeals to every sensitive ear and heart. Nevertheless, there are many who wish to understand and learn the basics of different styles of music. Over the last three decades there has been a growing interest in Hindustani classical music in the southern part of India (which has its own music system known as Carnatic system) and also abroad. The words like *sitār, sarod, rāg, tāl,* etc. are well known in several Western countries.

The present book is intended for those who are desirous of obtaining a reasonably sufficient knowledge of the fundamentals of Hindustani classical music in a relatively small span of time, without entering into the intricacies of the subject which are not of immediate use for a beginner.

The evolution of Hindustani music involves a lengthy and complex process extended over the past many thousand years. As such, it encompasses huge amount of literature giving information on various aspects of the subject. It was, therefore, a difficult task to condense a great deal of material into a comparatively small space and at the same time incorporate all the essential features of the Hindustani classical music. It was felt that no useful purpose would be served by giving a detailed account of the antiquated terms and styles of singing; hence attempts were made to make the subject matter easy-to-use and contemporary. Examples have been given to make the subject intelligible even to those who had earlier, no formal exposure to Hindustani music.

One important decision that was to be taken was regarding the spelling and pronunciation of the Hindi terms and names used in this book. One option was to adopt the spellings which are generally used. But such spellings resulted in pronunciations different from those in Hindi. Here we can consider a familiar example of the Hindi word *yog*. If it is spelt as *yoga*, as is generally done, its pronunciation would be quite different than that in Hindi. The word *yoga* in Hindi is pronounced as "yolk" in English where "lk" is replaced by "g." It was, therefore, decided that the Hindi words should be spelt in such a way that their utterances are phonetically, as close as possible, to those in Hindi. In doing so, certain simple symbols have been used which have been listed immediately after the preface. It is absolutely a must that the readers thoroughly study these before reading the book.

The present book comprises seven chapters. The first chapter gives a brief account of the history and evolution of the Hindustani music in a chronological order. The second and third chapters deal with various terms and processes involved in the performance of Hindustani classical vocal music. An account of various *gharānā*s of vocal music and life-histories of some eminent musicologists and singers is the subject matter of the fourth and fifth chapters. Vocal music is always enriched when accompanied by certain musical instruments; these have been described in the sixth chapter. The seventh and the last chapter is devoted to the description of certain famous *rāg*s which are frequently presented in musical concerts these days.

Efforts have been made to present the subject in a very simple manner using easy language so that even beginners can conveniently use this book. It should be useful to those also who cannot go through voluminous treatises on the subject due to paucity of time.

While, and in, writing this book my husband Ashish and daughter Vishakha showed great patience and co-operated with me – my sincere thanks to them.

Finally I wish to thank Mr Susheel K. Mittal of D.K. Printworld (P) Ltd., New Delhi for his co-operation in efficient and timely publication of this work.

I take this opportunity to express my deepest sense of gratitude to my *guru* Padmabhushan Dr K.J. Yesudas for his inspiration and encouragement to learn more — a process I hope will continue throughout my life.

The author would welcome any suggestions for improving this book.

**Shruti Jauhari**

# About Pronunciation of Hindi Words

HINDI terms, when written in English, have limitations in terms of phonetics. In this book, various Hindi terms have been presented in a symbolised manner, which help pronouncing these terms close to their utterances in Hindi. Consider the following examples:

1. About the use of vowel "a"

   (a) The vowel "a" is never to be pronounced as that in the English word "cat."

   (b) The vowel "a" is to be emphasised when there is a bar above, i.e. ā. For example, in the Hindi word *rāg*, "a" will be pronounced just as in the English word "car." If this is followed, the utterance of *rāg* will be just like that in Hindi.

   (c) In certain Hindi words, the vowel "a" is used in two ways. In some cases there is a greater emphasis on a particular "a" which has been shown by ā, for example, in the word

| M | a | h | ā | b | h | ā |
|---|---|---|---|---|---|---|
| r | a | t | | | | |
| | 1 | | 2 | | | 3 |
| | 4 | | | | | |

"a"s marked 2 and 3 are to be emphasised (as in car) but not those marked 1 and 4, although both the varieties of "a" have the same accent. The vowel "a" without any symbol is to be pronounced as "a" in the English word "rural" or "neutral".

(d) The use of the vowel "a" at the end of certain words has been omitted as it makes their pronunciations quite different from those in Hindi. Let us consider the examples given in Table A.

**Table A**

| Spellings Generally in Use | Spellings Used in the Present Book |
|---|---|
| Ashoka | Ashok |
| Buddha | Buddh |
| nāda | nāḍ |
| rāga | rāg |
| Rāma | Rām |
| svara | svar |
| tāla | tāl |
| tāna | tān |

The pronunciations of words written in the second column of Table A are closer to their utterances in Hindi.

(e) In a few cases, the conditions given in points 1(a) to 1(d) have been relaxed for the reasons given below:

(i) The Hindi word *lay* means tempo. [Here it should be remembered that "a" in this word is not to be pronounced as in the word "cat," see point 1 (a).] It has been spelt as *laya* to avoid confusion with the English word "lay". In the Hindi word *laya*, the "a" at the end is practically silent; this has been indicated by an underscore, i.e. *laya̲*.

(ii) The Hindi term *śāstr* has been written as *śāstra̲* as the non-Hindi-speaking people will find it difficult to utter *śāstr*. For similar reason, in the words given in Table B, the vowel "a" at the end has been retained but underlined to depict that it is practically silent.

**Table B**

| | |
|---|---|
| **alpatv** | *has been written as* **alpatva̲** |
| **āśray** | *has been written as* **āśraya̲** |
| **bahutv** | *has been written as* **bahutva̲** |
| **lay** | *has been written as* **laya̲** |
| **mandr** | *has been written as* **mandra̲** |
| **madhy** | *has been written as* **madhya̲** |
| **nāṭy** | *has been written as* **nāṭya̲** |
| **śāstr** | *has been written as* **śāstra̲** |
| **śiṣy** | *has been written as* **śiṣya̲** |
| **vādy** | *has been written as* **vādya̲** |

2. Table C gives guidance on the pronunciation of different letters or combination of letters used in the Hindi words, e.g. "e" should be pronounced as "ay" in the English word "say".

**Table C**

| | |
|---|---|
| **a** | as "a" in **rural** |
| **ā** | as "a" in **car** |
| **a̲** | "a" is **silent** |
| **e** | as "ay" in **say** |
| **ee/(ī)** | as "ee" in **need** |
| **i** | as "i" in **give** |
| **o** | as "o" in **go** |

| | |
|---|---|
| **oo/ū** | as "oo" in **t<u>oo</u>** |
| **u** | as "u" in **put** |
| **ai** | as "y" in **cycle** |
| **au** | as "au" in **<u>au</u>ra** |
| **ou** | as "ou" in **ab<u>ou</u>t** |
| **bh** | as "bh" in **a<u>bh</u>or** |
| **ch** | as "ch" in **<u>ch</u>urch** |
| **dh** | as "dh" in **<u>dh</u>arma** (adopted from Hindi) |
| **gh** | as "gh" in **<u>gh</u>ost** |
| **kh** | as "kh" in **<u>kh</u>an** |
| **ph** | as "ph" in **<u>ph</u>armacy** |
| **th** | as "th" in **<u>th</u>ought** |
| **ḍ** | as "d" in **<u>d</u>oll** |
| **d** | pronounced softly as **"the"** |
| **ṁ** | as "um" in **p<u>um</u>p** |
| **ṅ** | as "un" in **s<u>ung</u>** |
| **ṇ** | as "un" in **f<u>un</u>d** |
| **sh (ś)** | as "sh" in **<u>sh</u>arp** |
| **ṛ/ri** | as "ri" in **<u>ri</u>ch** |
| **ṣ** | as "sh" in **thra<u>sh</u>** |
| **ṭ** | as "t" in **<u>t</u>all** |
| **t** | pronounced softly |
| **ṭh** | no equivalent in English words |
| **chh** | no equivalent in English words |
| **kṣ/kṣa** | no equivalent in English words |

3. The spellings of a few frequently used common words like Hindi, Urdu, Hindu and Hindustani have not

been changed to Hindī, Urdū, Hindū and Hindustānī. The prevalent spellings are quite familiar and are correctly pronounced. Any change in their spellings would have made the user rather uncomfortable.

**Table D**

| Singular Form | Plural Form |
|---|---|
| *alaṁkār* | *alaṁkār*s |
| *bol* | *bol*s |
| *palṭā* | *palṭā*s |
| *rāg* | *rāg*s |
| *ṛṣī* | *ṛṣī*s |
| *saptak* | *saptak*s |
| *śruti* | *śruti*s |
| *svar* | *svar*s |
| *tāl* | *tāl*s |
| *tān* | *tān*s |
| *tānpūrā* | *tānpūrā*s |
| *thāṭ* | *thāṭ*s |
| *varṇa* | *varṇa*s |
| *vīṇā* | *vīṇā*s |

4. In order to convert Hindi terms from their singular to plural form, "s" has been added as shown in Table D. However, this addition of "s" is not in italic.

5. A list of terms and names used in this book has been given in Appendices I to V.

# Contents

# 1

# A Brief History of Hindustani Music

## 1.1 The Origin of Indian Music

EVER since the evolution of mankind, vocal music, that is singing, has been one of the natural and powerful media of expression of emotions. There are a number of theories regarding the origin of Indian music. According to one popular view, Brahmā created music and passed it to Śiva̱.[1] It is Sarasvatī, recognised as the Goddess of music and literature, who acquired the same from Śiva̱. However, the most ancient theory is that Lord Śiva̱ is the Supreme Deity of dance, drama and music. A similar situation exists about the period when the Indian music came into being. As per ancient Hindu scriptures music has been in existence since the last several thousand years. Archaeological evidence suggests that music existed during Indus-Valley Civilisation some 2500 years before Christ. Since then Indian music had undergone complex and varied interactions between different people of different races and cultures before acquiring its present form. Now, as music is a performing art, it is not possible to record its status at different stages of its evolution. However, there is ample material in ancient texts about the classification and description of various *rāgs*:

1. Brahmā, Viṣṇu and Śiva̱ are the three supreme gods of Hindus.

this is how this ancient art is known even today. The development of Indian music can be divided roughly into different periods as shown further.

### 1.2 The Ancient Period (2500–1500 BCE)

Little is known about the music of the Indus-Valley Civilisation. However, some musical instruments, such as the arched or bow-shaped string instrument (harp) and a variety of drums identified from the terracotta figures obtained during excavations in Moheṅjo-Daṛo and Haṛappā (now in Pakistan), provide a definite evidence for the existence of music during that period.

### 1.3 The Vedic Period (1500–500 BCE)

With the advent of the Āryans,[2] the Vedic culture[3] dominated all forms of learning. The priests composed hymns (*r̥chās*) in praise of gods which were sung in a well-defined style and thus evolved the Vedic music which was totally devoted to *bhakti*:[4] this was known as *Mārgī Saṅgīt*.[5] It was developed by great sages or *r̥ṣis* who were supposed to possess supernatural powers, hence no modifications in their compositions were permitted. Vedic music was purely religious in nature. Apart from singing, it also incorporated musical instruments such as *vīṇā*, *mr̥daṅg*, *vaṅśī*, etc. Music was passed on in a tradition known as *guru*[6]-*śiṣya*[7] *paramparā*[8]

2. An ancient Hindu race.
3. Āryan culture.
4. Devotion to God.
5. Celestial music.
6. Teacher.
7. Student.
8. Tradition.

in which there was a direct transfer of knowledge from the teacher to his students at the *gurukul* (teacher's residence).

Out of the four Vedas,[9] the *Sāmaveda* contains hymns which are to be chanted in a musical form. As such this Veda is directly connected to music. Prior to *Sāmaveda* only three musical notes, namely *udātt, anudātt* and *svarit* were used. The musical chanting of the *Sāmaveda* used more notes or *svars*, finally employing seven notes which turned out to be the basis of Indian classical music.

### 1.4 Music in Rāmāyaṇ and Mahābhārat (500–300 BCE)

The most popular epic *Rāmāyaṇ* was written in *śloka* form by the sage Vālmīki. The term *śloka* means a particular metrical composition chanted in easy tempo. There are several descriptions of singing and the use of musical instruments such as *vīṇā, dundubhi, bherī, mṛdaṅg*, etc. in *Rāmāyaṇ*. The demon-king Rāvaṇ and the monkey-king Sugrīv were proficient in music. As *Rāmāyaṇ* was sung rather than read, it helped music in entering every Indian household. Another great epic written after *Rāmāyaṇ* was *Mahābhārat* which was composed by Kṛṣṇadvaipāyan (Vyās). The *Mahābhārat* consisted of about one lakh *ślokas* and was supposed to be written around 400 BCE. Musicology during this period was referred to as *Gandharva śāstra*. *Gandharvas*[10] and *apsarases*[11] were great experts in singing and dancing. The hero of *Mahābhārat* "Arjun" was proficient in dance and music which he learnt from *gandharva* king Chitrasen. Kings maintained music schools for training of princesses and others. The use of music in festivals was an essential feature thereby bringing about the fact that

9. Religious treatises of Hindus.
10. Celestial musicians.
11. Celestial female dancers.

music was important to human life even during *Rāmāyaṇ* period.

### *1.4.1 Music in Jain[12] and Buddhist Literature*

Buddh was born in 563 BCE, around the time when classical music was in its prime position. It has been mentioned that an orchestra of 500 instruments was arranged to celebrate the birth ceremony of Buddh. The artists appointed to conduct musical prayers in *bauddha-vihārs*[13] were suitably rewarded and encouraged by the government. In Jain texts certain musical instruments have been described which are not mentioned elsewhere.

## 1.5 The Period of 300 BCE – CE 300

Indian mythology regards music to be of divine origin. It is believed that the celestial sage Nārad was the first to realise the laws of music. But the literature on music and drama (*nāṭya̲*) appeared much later. The famous book *Nāṭyaśāstra̲* written by Bharat sometime between 200 BCE and CE 200 deals with rules for theatre, music and dance. This treatise also describes different types of musical instruments in great detail. This book was of immense value for the students of music and theatre for several years to follow.

Purāṇa̲s[14] have also highlighted the importance of music in human life. In Purāṇa̲s, receiving of musical knowledge is regarded as a divine boon.

Around the third and fourth centuries the long process of development of music culminated in the arrangement of

---

12. An Indian religion.
13. Buddhist temples.
14. Mythological treatises of Hindus.

*svars* (musical notes) into definite order or pattern, thus giving rise to various *rāgs*.

### *1.5.1 Music in Maurya̲ Period*

Chandragupta̲ Maurya̲ was a renowned king who took interest in promoting music. But this was the period when music was gradually deviating from its religious form. People started thinking that music should enrich their life by providing entertainment. Rich people arranged musical *baiṭhak* (sittings) at their place to entertain their guests. During this period, i.e. around 300 BCE, the marriage of Chandragupta̲ took place with the daughter of Seleucus who was the chief commander of the Roman army of Alexander The Great. This event inducted some Roman touch to Indian music. Chandragupta̲'s son Bindusār did not do much towards the development of music. But later, his son, the great king Aśok, made attempts to bring back the Indian classical music to its past glory. After embracing Buddhism, Aśok sent delegations to countries like Tibet, China, Japan, Sumatra, Java, Sri Lanka, etc. for the promotion of Buddhism — this also helped in spreading Indian music in major parts of Asia.

After Aśok, Indian music started declining but king Kaniṣka̲ (CE 125–162) who himself was a musician again made attempts to raise the standard of Indian music. He invited musicians not only from different parts of India but also from China, Afghanistan, etc. for musical gatherings. Thus Kaniṣka̲ can be credited with the unification of music throughout the country and promoting it in other countries as well.

## **1.6 The Gupta̲ Period (CE 300–600)**

In between Kaniṣka̲ and the Gupta̲ dynasty nothing significant could be done towards the development of music.

The Gupta̲ dynasty founded by Chandragupta̲ (CE 320-35) ruled India up to CE 540. The period of Gupta̲ kings is marked with a great degree of excellence in literature and other arts. In fact, this period is referred to as the "Golden Age of Culture."

Chandragupta̲ I spent most of his time in wars hence he could not pay much attention to music. But his son Samudragupta̲ was himself an expert *vīṇā* player. During his period there was a great qualitative improvement in music which was regarded as an important means of enriching human life.

The world-famous poet Kālidās was in the court of Vikramāditya̲ Chandragupta̲ II (CE 380–413). He was a lyrical poet and a writer of epic and plays. Amongst his famous creations are *Śākuntalam, Meghadūtam* and *Raghuvaṁśam.* There are several references to music and dance in Kālidās' works showing the importance accorded to music during his period.

It is said that the now-so-famous instrument *sitār* was the invention of this period. Folk music and dances were very popular. One must not forget that folk music played a very important role in framing the classical music so much so that many people believed that "*ras-yukt saṅgīt*[15] (melodious music called *deśī saṅgīt*)" evolved from folk music. Historians opine that there was much more development and refinement of music in the Gupta̲ period as compared to any other period of Indian history. Indian music was famous not only in neighbouring countries but also in European countries. Thus this period is correctly called the "Golden period" as far as music is concerned.

15. Music.

During this period music no longer remained purely *mārgī* (religious) but was amply used for entertainment (*deśī saṅgīt*) as well. Thus the long process of evolution of music had crystallised into music of *rāg*s. This involved musical thinking that aimed at meaningfully organising melodic and tonal material. *Dattilam* written by Dattil sometime around CE 400 was the main text which explained terms like *svar, śruti*, rearrangement of *svar*s (*mūrchhanā*), *tān*s, *rāg*s, etc.

### 1.7 The Period CE 600–1200: Deśī Music

As already mentioned, around CE 400, the *deśī* music started acquiring more and more attention and a need was felt for a text pertaining to *deśī saṅgīt* which was provided by Mataṅga who in the eighth century composed *Bṛhaddeśī* (the great treatise on the regional music). This was the first important text after Bharat's *Nāṭyaśāstra* and before the Islamic influence on Indian music. According to Mataṅga, *deśī saṅgīt* is that which comes out spontaneously and sung with delight and pleasure by anybody be it women, children, educated, illiterate, rich, poor, an individual, or a group of people in their region. The music thus evolved was then formulated and recorded in musical treatises for preservation and hence many *rāg*s came into being.

The present system of Indian music rests on two pillars, namely *rāg* and *tāl*. *Rāg* is melodic while *tāl* is rhythmic. The *rāg* and *tāl* combination of Indian music distinguishes it from any other musical system. Thus *rāg*, which means colour or passion, is essentially a framework of certain (5-7) musical notes or *svar*s which form a pleasing and rhythmic combination. The singer goes from one note to another in a characteristic manner — thus creating the atmosphere of the *rāg* in his own style. The idea of *tāl* is related to the concept of time. A singer marks the beginning from a particular point of time called *sam* and, after producing pleasing note-combinations, returns to the *sam* after one or more *āvartans*. A particular period of time is known as *āvartans*. Each *āvartan* is of equal time interval. The singing speed can be very slow, medium or fast depending upon the musical composition.

### *1.7.1 The Advent of Islam*

From CE 600 onwards India got divided into several states that fought with each other. People forgot to derive real pleasure from music. Competition between different states started. Different regions modified musicology according to their wish and thus many *gharānā*s or *sampradāyas*[16] came into being.

India was constantly under attack right from eighth century. Around ninth century, Sūfīs[17] who came along with Muslim invaders showed great interest in Indian music. But since they had no interest in *saṅgīt śāstras*,[18] they modified Indian music in a way they liked. Some people regard it as a deformation whereas some consider this phenomenon as an enrichment of Indian music. Unlike in the north, the south Indian music (Karnatic[19] music) could be preserved and practised freely.

## 1.8 The Khiljī Period (CE 1290–1320)

During this period a very talented musician Amīr Khusro invented many *rāg*s, *tāl*s and musical instruments. It is said that he was the person who developed *sitār* and *tablā*. He had full support from the state in his musical pursuit. He

16. Schools of music.
17. Muslim saints.
18. Treatises on music.
19. Karnatic music is the music system prevalent in south India.

served under many kings and was in contact with many Sūfīs too.

### 1.9 The Tughlaq Period (CE 1320–1400)

Gayāsuddīn Tughlaq had practically no interest in music but his son Mohammad Tughlaq was a music lover. He encouraged the musicians; however, in his regime there was no state support to musicians. Śāraṅgadev in the thirteenth century composed a very important treatise known as *Saṅgīt-Ratnākar* which is highly regarded both by Hindustani and Karnatic musicians.

### 1.10 The Lodhī Period (CE 1450–1525)

Sikandar Lodhī had no knowledge of music but he had respect for musicians. During this period the Hindu music lovers wanted to retain the Indian traditions in music, whereas the Muslims wanted to give it a Persian form. The Muslim influence on music gave rise to new styles of singing such as *ṭhumrī, kawwālī, khayāl, ghazal,* etc. The king of Jaunpur Sultān Hussain Śarqī patronized the *khayāl* style of singing in 1500.

### 1.11 The Mughal Period (CE 1525–1740)

Bābur had some knowledge of music and he would reward musicians but, for him music was only for entertainment. Humāyūṅ, Bābur's son, was too busy in wars to find any time for music. During this period the king of Gwalior Rājā Mānsingh Tomar encouraged the *Dhrupad*[20] style of singing in order to preserve Indian traditional music. Sūfī music was becoming more and more dominating as it had state patronage. Parallel to this, *bhakti-saṅgīt* (devotional music) was also coming up: great saints such as Sūrdās, Haridās, Mīrā,

20. *Dhrupad* was an ancient style of singing. Rājā Mānsingh had developed the contemporary form of *dhrupad*.

Tulsīdās inducted a new life in Indian music during its difficult times.

The *bhakti* cult during the fourteenth and fifteenth centuries revolved around Rām and Kṛṣṇa̱.[21] Theoreticians like Rāmānujāchārya̱ and Rāmānand and saint poets like Kabīr and Tulsīdās belonged to the Rām tradition. Vallabhāchārya̱, Chaitanya̱ and others belonged to Kṛṣṇa̱ tradition. The Vallabha̱ followers immensely contributed to Indian music. Several saints in different parts of India contributed to the *bhakti* movement: some of these were Jaidev, Vidyāpati, Chaṇḍīdās, Narsiṁha̱ Bhagat, etc. *Havelī saṅgīt* was the temple music practised in Nāthdwārā in Rajasthan.[22]

### *1.11.1 The Period of Akbar (CE 1560–1605)*

Prior to Akbar the political situation of India was rather unstable. Wars were frequent and the Mughal Dynasty was not firmly established. In the field of music also there was chaos. *Bhakti-saṅgīt, Sūfī-saṅgīt, dhrupad-dhamār, khayāl, ṭhumrī, kawwālī* — all the musical styles were being followed. By the end of the sixteenth century the Mughal empire was firmly established by Akbar. During his regime there was a lot of progress in the field of art and music. There were several eminent musicians in his court, Tānsen being the most famous. Tānsen was previously in the court of the king of Rīwā. He was such a fine singer that Akbar invited him to his court. His original name was Tannā Miśrā and he belonged to a brāhmaṇa̱[23] family of Gwalior. It is said that another great singer of that time known as Baijū Nāyak defeated Tānsen in a musical competition. Swāmī Haridās of

21. Hindu gods.
22. A north-western state of India.
23. Upper caste Hindus.

Brindāvan was a very great saint-singer who had taught music both to Tānsen and Baijū. This great saint was contemporary to Mīrā, Tulsīdās and Sūrdās.

After Akbar, his son Jahāṅgīr became the king. He was a lover of music. During his time musical concerts were arranged and musicians were rewarded. The musicians were quite rich and prosperous but they had little interest in the theoretical aspect of music and distorted the traditional music in order to please their patrons. Moreover, they would sell their knowledge and even their religion. Jahāṅgīr's son Shahjahān was also an admirer of music who used to give valuable gifts to artists. Around 1660, Aurangzeb became the ruler. He never realised the true form of music and therefore was against music.

### 1.12 The Decline of Mughal Dynasty

Mohammad Shāh Raṅgīle (CE 1720–1740) was the last Mughal ruler. He himself was a good musician and encouraged music performers. In his court, there were three musicians who very profoundly contributed to *khayāl* singing: they were Adāraṅg, Sadāraṅg and Mahāraṅg (*khayāl* singing was first introduced by the king of Jaunpur in CE 1500). Towards the end of the Mughal Dynasty *khayāl, ṭhumrī, dādrā, ghazals, ṭappā,* etc. had become extremely popular and *dhrupad-dhamār* was rarely heard.

### 1.13 The British Period

Around 1850 the British had control over a major part of the country. British administrators considered Indian music uncivilised and always neglected it. The Indian music during this period, therefore, was in the hands of low class people. People of good standing hesitated to send their children to music schools.

## 1.14 Music in Modern India (CE 1900 Onwards)

The invaluable contribution of two great music promoters, namely Pandit[24] V.N. Bhatkhande and Pandit V.D. Paluskar will always be remembered for reviving the Indian classical music in independent India. Before the advent of Muslims, the art of music was mainly with brāhmaṇa̲s and was restricted to temples and royal courts. During the Muslim period although the ancient Indian music was greatly distorted at the same time it was made much more popular and was practised and enjoyed by all sections of the society. Consequently, this degenerated the standard of music and allowed the entry of low class people into the field of music. This was the reason why during the eighteenth and nineteenth centuries, the people from civilised families kept their family members away from the art of music. Under such circumstances, Bhatkhande and Paluskar made marathon efforts to revive the Indian classical music. They toured extensively to collect musical literature and developed notations for describing different *rāg*s. They met most of the eminent singers of the time and obtained from them the details of as many *rāg*s as possible. All this information was transformed into the notation system and then published in the form of several books. They also arranged several musical concerts, established "All India Music Academy" and started many music colleges.

India became an independent country in 1947. The national Government took a keen interest in resurrecting Indian art and culture. The then Information and Broadcasting Minister B.V. Ḳeskar gave much importance to programmes on Indian classical music. The learned and great musicians were now honoured with the highest awards

24. Expert.

such as *Bhārat Ratna*. Many music colleges have been started and music has been introduced as a subject in many educational institutions. Indira Kala Sangeet University at Khairāgaṛh, M.P., is totally devoted to music and dance. In many universities researches are done in the field of music. During the twentieth century film music also played a major role in spreading Indian music to every corner of the country and abroad. Several talented film music directors have made an excellent use of Indian classical music in their compositions.

# 2

# Svar, Rāg and Tāl

In Indian music system, *nād* or *dhvani* (sound) is of utmost importance so much so that it is regarded as equivalent to God (*Nād-Brahma̱*). It is believed that through *nād* one can link himself with the supreme power, that is, God.

## 2.1 Sound: Its Production and Propagation

Sound is a form of energy which produces a sensation of hearing. Sound is produced as a result of vibration of a body. For example, when a stretched string is plucked, the string starts vibrating, thereby producing sound as we note in the case of guitar, *vīṇā* or *sitār*. Similarly, when a drum is struck with a stick, its surface starts vibrating which induces periodic motion in the surrounding air producing what are known as "sound waves." These waves strike our eardrums from where they reach a specific part of the brain through nerves and produce the sensation of sound.

Sound is produced by vibrating objects. Sound cannot travel through vacuum but needs a medium for its propagation. The matter through which sound is transmitted is called medium which can be solid, liquid or gas. This medium should be elastic and continuous. A vibrating body induces vibrations in the particles of the medium, which are in its immediate contact. Vibrations mean a kind of rapid to and fro motion of an object, say a pendulum.

A sound producing body, during its vibrations, makes a forward and then a backward movement continuously from its normal position (see *fig.* 2.1). When it moves forward, it pushes forward a particle of the medium which is in its immediate vicinity. This particle, in turn, pushes forward another particle adjacent to it and then moves itself back. This process initiates and propagates a chain in which the particles of the medium perform to and fro motion (vibration) continuously right from the source of the sound up to the ears of a listener. It is important to note that the particles of the medium do not move from the sound producing body to our ears but simply perform to and fro motion about their normal position, in the direction of wave motion.

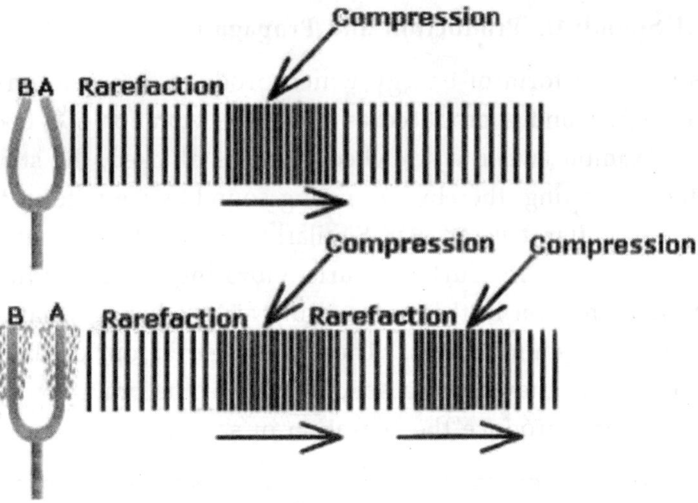


*fig.* 2.1: A vibrating object creating a series of compressions and rarefactions in the medium

Air is the most common medium through which sound travels. When a sound producing vibrating object moves forward (see *fig.* 2.1) it pushes and thereby compresses the air in front of it and forms what is called a compression zone. This compression zone starts moving away from the vibrating object. When the vibrating object moves backwards, it creates a low pressure zone in front of it, which is known as a rarefaction zone. Since pressure is directly proportional to density, the air density is greater in the compression zone than that in the rarefaction zone as shown in *fig*. 2.1.

As the vibrating object moves to and fro rapidly, a series of alternate compressions and rarefactions is generated in the air (see *fig*. 2.2). This constitutes a sound wave which transmits the sound through the air from the source to the listener. Thus a sound wave is a disturbance that moves through the medium as a result of oscillation of its particles. Here, the particles oscillate in a direction parallel to the direction of movement of the sound wave. These waves are known as longitudinal waves. Thus a sound wave is a longitudinal mechanical wave, which consists of a series of compression and rarefaction travelling through the medium. The propagation of sound through air can be visualized in terms of variation of pressure (or density) in the air (see *fig*. 2.2).

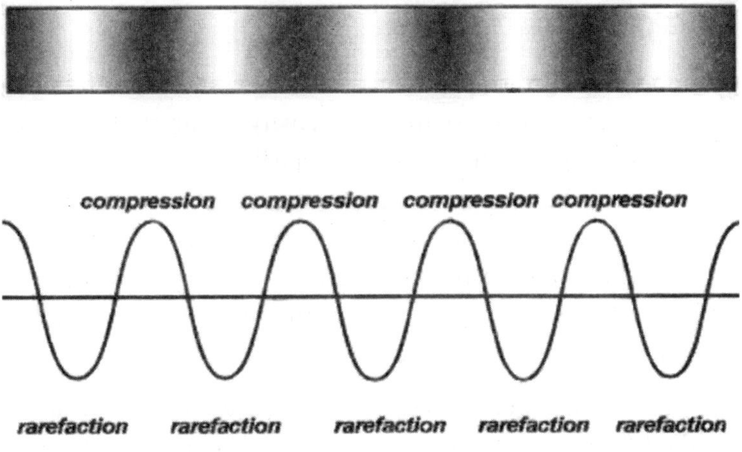


*fig*. 2.2: Variation in air pressure during propagation of sound

A sound wave in air is represented graphically by plotting pressure or density of air against distance from the source as shown in *fig.* 2.3:

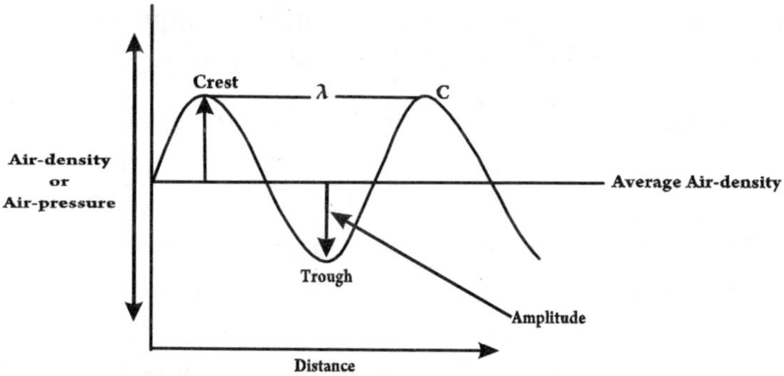


*fig.* 2.3: Graphical representation of a sound wave

## 2.2 Characteristics of a Sound Wave

A sound wave can be described by the following terms:

(a) Wavelength
(b) Frequency
(c) Speed or velocity
(d) Amplitude

### *2.2.1 Wavelength*

A sound wave in graphic form has been shown in *fig.* 2.3, which depicts how pressure and density of air change when a sound wave passes through it. The peak in *fig.* 2.3 represents the region of maximum compression where the pressure as well as density of the air is the maximum; this peak is called "crest." The valley in the curve shows the region where the air pressure and the air density is the minimum; this valley is known as "trough" of the wave.

The distance between two consecutive crests or troughs is called "wavelength" and is represented by the Greek letter λ (pronounced lambda). The maximum disturbance is called "amplitude."

### 2.2.2 *Frequency*

The number of wavelengths passing through a given point in one second is known as the "frequency" of the wave which is represented by the Greek letter $\nu$ (pronounced nu). The wavelength of a wave is inversely proportional to its frequency: this means greater the wavelength, smaller is the frequency. The unit of frequency is Hertz (Hz). One Hertz means one vibration per second, i.e. one wavelength passing through a point in one second.

Our ears are normally sensitive to only those vibrations whose frequency lies between 20 to 20,000; this frequency range, i.e. 20 Hz to 20k Hz (Kilo Hertz) is therefore called "audible range." When the frequency of sound waves is more than 20k Hz, it normally does not affect our ears and hence cannot be heard. Such waves are referred to as "ultrasonic waves." On the other hand, waves having frequency less than 20 Hz, are also not audible; these are called "infrasonic waves."

### 2.2.3 *Speed or Velocity of Sound*

Sound waves need a medium for their propagation. In different kinds of media these waves have different speeds. The product of the wavelength and frequency of a wave gives the value of its velocity (c) : i.e. $\lambda \times \nu = c$.

### 2.2.4 *Amplitude*

A sound wave is a disturbance that moves through a medium as a result of the oscillations of its particles. Greater the extent of disturbance, greater is the intensity of the sound produced. The magnitude of maximum disturbance in the medium is called "amplitude" of the wave which has been shown in *fig.* 2.5(B). The value of the amplitude of the wave governs the intensity of the sound (see *fig.* 2.5). It can be noted that in *fig*. 2.5(A), the amplitude is small, hence the intensity of sound will be small while in *fig*. 2.5(B), the amplitude is comparatively large, hence in this case the sound intensity will be greater.

### 2.3 Characteristics of Sound

Sound has three important characteristics, namely pitch, intensity and timbre.

#### *2.3.1 Pitch of a Sound*

A woman's voice is finer or thinner than that of a man. In scientific language, we can say that the pitch or the frequency of the voice of a woman is higher than that of a man. It means that higher the pitch of a sound, greater will be the frequency of the associated sound wave as shown in *fig*. 2.4.

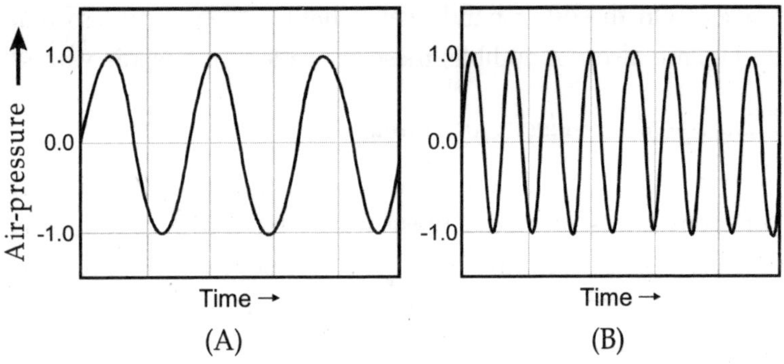


*fig*. 2.4: (A): Low frequency sound wave has low pitch
(B): High frequency sound wave has high pitch

#### *2.3.2. Intensity of a Sound*

The intensity of a sound is determined by the magnitude of the amplitude of the associated wave. Greater the amplitude greater is the intensity or the loudness of the sound and vice versa (see *fig*. 2.5).

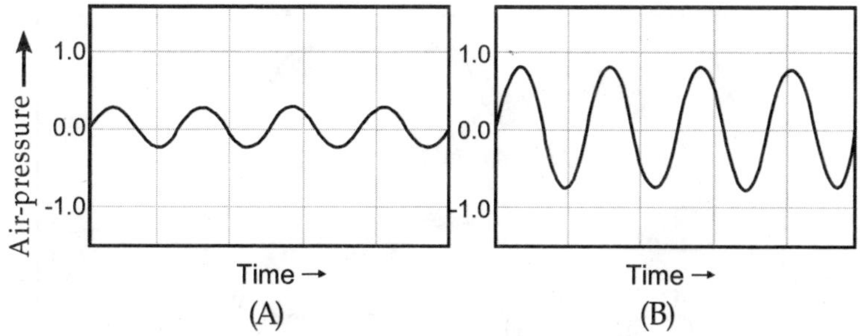


*fig.* 2.5: (A): Small amplitude has soft sound
(B): Large amplitude has loud sound

### *2.3.3 Timbre*

The quality or timbre of sound is that characteristic which enables us to distinguish one kind of sound from another having the same pitch and loudness. For example, we can always know whether it is human voice or sound coming from a harmonium or a flute or a *sitār*.

The important points to remember are:

1. The intensity of a sound depends upon the amplitude of the sound wave, and
2. The pitch of a sound depends upon the frequency of the sound wave.

### *2.3.4 Musical and Non-Musical Sound*

Musical sound involves a sound wave that is regular and of a fixed frequency like the one shown in *fig.* 2.6A.

The uniform and regular sound of a fixed frequency in musical language is called *nād* (*fig.* 2.6A). The *nād* has a characteristic sound or quality from which we can make out whether it is coming from a harmonium or *vīṇā* or *mr̥daṅg*[1] or is a human voice. The quality of sound is referred to as "timbre."

1. Musical instruments.

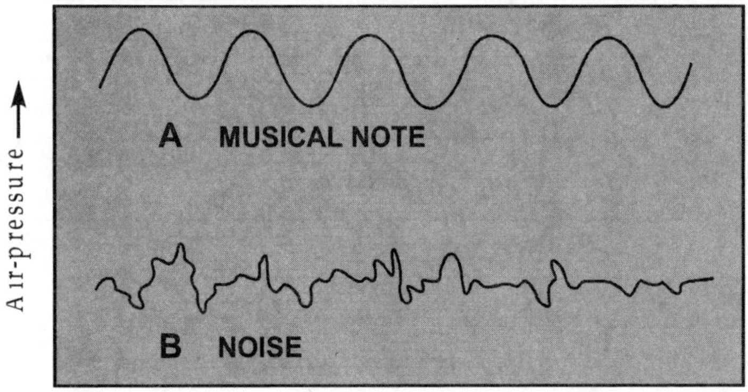


*fig.* 2.6: A : Uniform and regular sound wave
B : Non-uniform and irregular sound wave

Non-musical sound, called "noise," is one which consists of non-uniform and irregular waves, i.e. sound of different volumes and frequencies (*fig.* 2.6B). Such a sound is not useful for musical activities.

## 2.4 Anāhat and Āhat-nād

*Anāhat-nād* is abstract and is not produced by friction or by striking an object. Sages or *ṛṣi*s experience this during meditation. This type of *nād* is not used for any musical purpose.

*Āhat-nād* is one which is produced as a result of friction such as that of a bow on a violin or when we strike a body such as that in a piano. The resulting sound has a fixed pitch and a good quality or timbre. Only such sound is useful from music point of view.

## 2.5 Śruti and Svar

Sound which can be distinguished from another sound or *nād* is called *śruti*. For example, consider a wire stretched between two fixed points. When it is plucked, it vibrates giving a *nād* of frequency, say, 240 (per second). If there is another similar wire vibrating with frequency 241, it is not possible to differentiate between the two *nād*s by human ear. If the frequency of the second wire is increased gradually, a stage will come when the *nād* produced by it will appear to be different from that of the first wire. Since the two *nād*s are now discernible, they will be referred to as *śruti*s.

If we have a wire vibrating with frequency 240 and another with frequency 480, then there will be a "resonance" between the *nād*s produced by the two vibrating wires. In between these two *nād*s, Indian musicologists have identified 22 *nād*s which can be distinguished from one another and are used in music: these are *śruti*s. In fact, nobody can use all 22 *śruti*s during singing. Moreover, such a combination will not be pleasing to our ears. Hence, out of these 22 *śruti*s, 12 have been identified which are used while singing: these are known as *svar*s.[2] Basically there is no difference between *svar*s and *śruti*s. When one sings a *rāg* he uses certain *śruti*s which become *svar*s and others remain as *śruti*s. If he sings another *rāg*, then certain other *śruti*s may become *svar*s and *svar*s used in the previous *rāg* may now become *śruti*s. In going from one *svar* to another a versatile singer may use the *śruti*s lying in between the two *svar*s but the use of *śruti* will be for a very small fraction of a second whereas the *śruti* being used as a *svar* is prominently used and one can stay on it for a while.

In ancient India *svar*s of only three pitches were used during singing, namely:

| | |
|---|---|
| *udātta* | high |
| *anudātta* | low |
| *svarit* | in-between |

Later 7 and subsequently 12 *svar*s were used. Out of these, 7

2. *Svar*s means musical notes.

are called *śuddh* and 5 are known as *vikr̥t*. These *svars* or notes constitute what is known as a *saptak* or musical scale.

## 2.6 The Musical Scale (Svar Saptak)

The evolution of musical scale used in Hindustani classical music involved a lengthy and complicated mechanism. Here we shall try to understand the basic idea that helped the development of musical scale in brief.

### *2.6.1 Iṣṭatā and Aniṣṭatā*

When the combination of two notes (*svars*) is pleasant, they are said to be *iṣṭa̱* to each other and this phenomenon is called *iṣṭatā* (extreme liking for each other) or *saṁvād* or consonance. On the other hand, certain note-combinations sound unpleasant: this effect is called *aniṣṭatā* (disliking) or dissonance. As will be discussed later, there can be different degrees of consonance and dissonance.

Consider two *tānpūrās* (a musical instrument, see *fig.* 6.2) each having only one string and both tuned to the same *svar*. When both the *tānpūrās* are played simultaneously the resultant sound will be richer and pleasant. Now one of the *tānpūrās* is kept as such, while the tension of the wire in the second *tānpūrā* is slightly increased so that its frequency becomes slightly greater than that of the wire in the first *tānpūrā*. As this is done, the combination of the sound produced by the two *tānpūrās* will become unpleasant. If the tension of the wire in the second *tānpūrā* is gradually increased, a series of pleasant and unpleasant sounds will be heard when the two *tānpūrās* are played simultaneously. Such observations played an important role in the development of the Indian musical scale.

From very early times Indian musicologists recognised that the combination of notes of frequencies in the ratio 2:3

produce a very pleasant effect which they termed *saṁvād*. For example, a wire vibrating with a frequency of 240 oscillations per second will establish *saṁvād* (consonance) with that vibrating at 360. This is how the first note called *ṣaḍja̱* (Ṡā or S in the symbolic form) and the fifth note *pañcham* (Pa or P) of the Indian musical scale were located. These two *svar*s produce what is known as *ṣaḍja̱-pañcham bhāv* (relation or mood). Likewise, the frequency ratio 320:480 also produced *saṁvād*.

The *ṣaḍja̱* having frequency 480 is known as *tār ṣaḍja̱* depicted as Ṡā. The note having frequency 320 is called *madhyam* which is denoted by Ma. In this way four *svar*s of the octave could be searched out. The study of the following examples will help in understanding the development of the Indian musical scale.

(i) A stretched wire is vibrating with a frequency 100 per second and another with 200. If both the wires are simultaneously plucked, the resultant sound will be richer and pleasant. Same will be the case with wires having frequencies 240 and 480 respectively.

(ii) Two wires vibrating with frequencies 240 and 360 respectively will be *ati-iṣṭa̱* to each other or there will be *ati-iṣṭatā* (great liking) between them. This *ati-iṣṭatā* is also known as *saṁvād* (consonance). It may be noted that in this case the frequency ratio is 2:3.

(iii) Frequency ratio 240:320 (3:4) is also a case of *ati-iṣṭatā* or *saṁvād*. It is known as *ṣaḍja̱–madhyam-bhāv.*

(iv) It was observed that frequency ratio 3:5 and 4:5 also gave rise to the pleasant sound but not as pleasant as in the examples (ii) and (iii). These ratios correspond to what is known as ordinary or normal *iṣṭatā* (normal liking) or *anuvād*.

(v) The frequency ratios 5:6 and 5:8 also have *iṣṭatā* but to a smaller extent, hence these are the cases of *alp-iṣṭatā* (small liking).

(vi) When the frequency ratio is 8:9, the combination of two notes sounds unpleasant. The phenomenon is therefore called *aniṣṭatā* (disliking) or *vivād.*

(vii) The frequency ratio 15:16 results in a very unpleasant sound. It is, therefore, referred to as *ati-aniṣṭatā* (extreme disliking).

The aforementioned observations have been summarised below:

| *Frequency ratio between two notes* | *Resultant note-combination is known as* | *Symbols of the corresponding note-combination in the musical scale (See Tables 2.1 and 2.3)* |
|---|---|---|
| 2:3 and 3:4 | *ati-iṣṭatā* | Sā-Pa and Sā-Ma |
| 3:5* and 4:5* | *iṣṭatā* | Sā-Dha and Sā-Ga |
| 5:6 and 5:8* | *alp-iṣṭatā* | Sā-Ga and Sā-Dha |
| 8:9 | *aniṣṭatā* | Sā-Re |
| 15:16* | *ati-aniṣṭatā* | Sā-Re |

* Approximately

While studying the relation between the different notes (*svars*) of the Indian musical scale (*saptak*), the following points should be kept in mind.

(a) The *aniṣṭatā* would be noted only when the two notes involved are simultaneously played on a musical instrument.

(b) The two *svars* of a *saptak* may be *aniṣṭ* to each other, but they do have their corresponding *iṣṭa svar* in the lower and higher *saptaks* (*mandra* and *tār saptak* — see Table 2.3).

(c) From the above and a few other considerations, 12 *svars* have been chosen from 22 *śrutis* that have been identified in one *saptak*: these have been shown in Table 2.1).

## 2.6.2 Relation between Śrutis, Svars and Frequencies

**Table 2.1**

| *No.* | *Śruti* | *Svar* | *Frequency* | *Keyboard Sign* |
|---|---|---|---|---|
| 1 | *Tīvrā* | Sā (*Achal*) | 240 | C |
| 2 | *Kumudvatī* | | | |
| 3 | *Mandā* | Re (*Komal*) | $254^{2}/17$ | C# |
| 4 | *Chhandovatī* | | | |
| 5 | *Dayāvatī* | Re (*Tīvra*) | 270 | D |
| 6 | *Ranjanī* | | | |
| 7 | *Ratikā* | Ga (*Komal*) | 288 | D# |
| 8 | *Raudrī* | Ga (*Tīvra*) | $301^{17}/43$ | E |
| 9 | *Krodhā* | | | |
| 10 | *Vajrikā* | Ma (*Komal*) | 320 | F |
| 11 | *Prasāriṇī* | Ma (*Tīvra*) | $338^{14}/17$ | F# |
| 12 | *Prīti* | | | |
| 13 | *Mārjnī* | | | |
| 14 | *Kṣiti* | Pa (*Achal*) | 360 | G |
| 15 | *Raktā* | Dha (*Komal*) | $381^{3}/17$ | G# |
| 16 | *Sandīpinī* | | | |
| 17 | *Ālāpinī* | | | |
| 18 | *Madantī* | Dha (*Tīvra*) | 405 | A |
| 19 | *Rohiṇī* | | | |

| | | | | |
|---|---|---|---|---|
| 20 | *Ramyā* | Ni (*Komal*) | 432 | A# |
| 21 | *Ugrā* | Ni (*Tīvra*) | $452^{4}/43$ | B |
| 22 | *Kṣobhiṇī* | | | |
| 1 | *Tīvrā* | Sā (*Tār*) | 480 | C |

*Note*: The frequencies of some of the notes in the Indian and Western system differ slightly.

Clarification of *svar*s given in Table 2.1:

1. *Svar*s "Sā" and "Pa" are fixed or *achal*. It means they are of only one kind which can be called *śuddh*.[3]

2. When the frequencies of Re, Ga, Dha and Ni are slightly decreased from their normal values we get their *komal* varieties which are represented by putting a line under them, i.e. Re, Ga, Dha and Ni respectively. When the frequencies are raised to their original values we get back the original *svar*s Re, Ga, Dha and Ni which represent the *śuddh* variety of these *svar*s, which are also called *tīvra svar*s or sharp notes.

3. In the case of *madhyam*, a new variety could not be obtained by slightly decreasing its frequency so it was itself taken as *śuddh*. However, on slightly increasing its frequency a new *svar* was identified which was given the name *tīvra madhyam*: this is represented as M̍a.

4. Certain authors of musical texts call *tīvra svar*s as *śuddh* and *komal svar*s as *vikṛt*.[4] But in the case of *madhyam* the situation is just the opposite, i.e. *komal* Ma is regarded as *śuddh* (represented as Ma without any line under it) and *tīvra* Ma is regarded as *vikṛt* and is represented by M̍a.

---

3. Pure.

4. Distorted.

The above discussion has been summarized in Table 2.2.

**Table 2.2**

| *No.* | *Symbol* | *Name of the Svar* |
|---|---|---|
| 1 | Sā or S | *Achal* or fixed — *ṣaḍja̲* |
| 2 | R̲e̲ or R̲ | *Komal* or *vikr̥t* — *r̥ṣabh* |
| 3 | Re or R | *Tīvra̲* or *śuddh* — *r̥ṣabh* |
| 4 | G̲a̲ or G̲ | *Komal* or *vikr̥t* — *gāndhār* |
| 5 | Ga or G | *Tīvra̲* or *śuddh* — *gāndhār* |
| 6 | Ma or M | *Komal* or *śuddh* — *madhyam* |
| 7* | M̍a or M̍ | *Tīvra̲* or *vikr̥t* — *madhyam* |
| 8 | Pa or P | *Achal* or fixed — *pañcham* |
| 9 | D̲h̲a̲ or D̲ | *Komal* or *vikr̥t* — *dhaivat* |
| 10 | Dha or D | *Tīvra̲* or *śuddh* — *dhaivat* |
| 11 | N̲i̲ or N̲ | *Komal* or *vikr̥t* — *niṣād* |
| 12 | Ni or N | *Tīvra̲* or *śuddh* — *niṣād* |

* Note the difference between *madhyam* and other *svars*.

## 2.7 Mandra̲, Madhya̲ and Tār Saptak

There are seven main *svars* in Hindustani classical music which form what is known as a *saptak*. Some details about these have been given in Table 2.3.

The *svars* 8 to 14 belong to the *madhya̲-saptak* in which the pitch is neither low nor high. *Svars* 15 to 21 belong to the *tār saptak*: here the pitch or the frequencies of the *svars* are higher as compared to those in the *madhya̲-saptak*. *Svars* number 1 to 7 constitute the *mandra̲-saptak* in which the pitch of the *svars* is lower than those in the *madhya̲-saptak*. It should be remembered that the frequency ratios between different *svars* remain unchanged irrespective of the *saptak* to which they belong.

**Table 2.3**

| *No.* | *Full name of the Svar* | Frequency | | *Symbol* | *(As per ancient text) Supposed to be originated from the voice of* |
|---|---|---|---|---|---|
| 1 | *Ṣaḍja* | 120 | Mandra–Saptak | Ṣ | |
| 2 | *Ṛṣabh* | | | Ṛ | |
| 3 | *Gāndhār* | | | G̣ | |
| 4 | *Madhyam* | | | Ṃ | |
| 5 | *Pañcham* | | | P̣ | |
| 6 | *Dhaivat* | | | Ḍ | |
| 7 | *Niṣād* | | | Ṇ | |
| 8 | *Ṣaḍja* | 240 | Madhya–Saptak | S | Peacock |
| 9 | *Ṛṣabh* | | | R | *Chātak* |
| 10 | *Gāndhār* | | | G | Goat |
| 11 | *Madhyam* | | | M | Crow |
| 12 | *Pañcham* | | | P | Cuckoo |
| 13 | *Dhaivat* | | | D | Frog |
| 14 | *Niṣād* | | | N | Elephant |
| 15 | *Ṣadja* | 480 | Tār–Saptak | Ṡ | |
| 16 | *Ṛṣabh* | | | Ṙ | |
| 17 | *Gāndhār* | | | Ġ | |
| 18 | *Madhyam* | | | Ṁ | |
| 19 | *Pañcham* | | | Ṗ | |
| 20 | *Dhaivat* | | | Ḋ | |
| 21 | *Niṣād* | | | Ṅ | |

### 2.7.1 *Ati-mandra̱ and Ati-tār Saptak*

Another *saptak* on the lower frequency range beyond *mandra̱-saptak* is known as *ati-mandra̱-saptak,* while the *saptak* beyond *tār-saptak* on the higher frequency side is called *ati-tār-saptak:* these have been shown below.

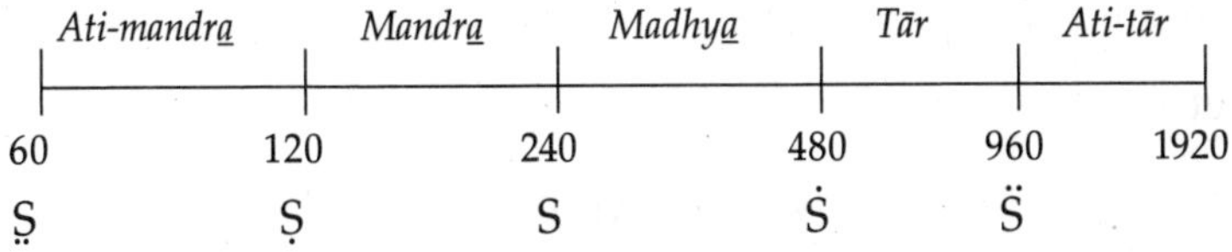


| *Name of the saptak* | *Symbol of the ṣaḍja̱ of the saptak* | *Frequency of the ṣaḍja̱* |
|---|---|---|
| *Ati-mandra̱* | S̤ | 60 |
| *Mandra̱* | Ṣ | 120 |
| *Madhya̱* | S | 240 |
| *Tār* | Ṡ | 480 |
| *Ati-tār* | S̈ | 960 |

In musical scale, the first note called *ṣaḍja̱* (denoted by Sā or S) is of utmost importance. Singers start their performance with this note. It is never forbidden in a *rāg* and given prominence in all the *rāgs*. This note should be regarded as the base note. The musical instruments, accompanying the singing process, such as *tablā, tānpūrā, sāraṅgī,* etc. are tuned in accordance with the frequency (or pitch) of the *ṣaḍja̱* used by the singer. In Table 2.3, the frequency of the *ṣaḍja̱* of the *madhya̱-saptak* has been taken as 240. But it is not essential that all the singers should sing in this particular pitch. The frequency of the *ṣaḍja̱* used by different singers is generally different. In fact, note (or *nād*) of any frequency, which a singer finds suitable, can be used as *ṣaḍja̱.* When the frequency of *ṣaḍja̱* is changed, the frequency of the other notes of the musical scale also changes proportionately.

## 2.8 Notations (as per Bhatkhande system)

If we write

S R G M P D N

It means that all the seven *svars* belong to the *madhya̲-saptak* and are *śuddh svars*.

Let us now consider the following example:

| Ṃ̍ D̲̣ Ṇ | S R̲ G M P D̲ N | Ṡ Ṙ Ġ̲ |
|---|---|---|
| *Mandra̲ saptak* | *Madhya̲ saptak* | *Tār saptak* |

From the above example, the following information can be obtained:

1. Ṃ̍ means *tīvra̲ madhyam*. Since there is a dot below it, this represents *tīvra̲ madhyam* of the *mandra̲ saptak*.
2. D̲ means *komal* D because there is a line below it. A dot has also been placed below D meaning it is of *mandra̲-saptak*. Thus D̲̣ represents *komal* (or *vikr̥t*) *dhaivat* of the *mandra̲-saptak*.
3. Ṇ is *śuddh* because there is no line below it. Since there is a dot below it, Ṇ means *śuddh* (or *tīvra̲*) *niṣād* of the *mandra̲-saptak*.
4. S and P are fixed or *achal*. Since there is no dot below or above them: these represent *ṣaḍja̲* and *pañcham* respectively of the *madhya̲ saptak*.
5. G and N represent *śuddh* (or *tīvra̲*) *gāndhār* and *niṣād* respectively because there is no line below them. Further there is no dot below or at the top of these *svars* so they cannot be in the *mandra̲* or *tār saptak*, hence these *svars* obviously should be of the *madhya̲-saptak*.

6. R̲ and D̲ represent *komal* (or *vikr̥t*) *r̥ṣabh* and *dhaivat* respectively. Since there is no dot below or at the top of these *svars*, they will belong to the *madhya̲-saptak.*
7. M represents *śuddh* or *komal madhyam* of the *madhya̲-saptak.*
8. Ṡ represents *tār-ṣaḍja̲* because there is a dot at the top of S.
9. Ṙ means *śuddh r̥ṣabh* of the *tār-saptak.*
10. Ġ̲ represents *komal gāndhār* in the *tār-saptak.*

The following examples are from *ati-tār* and *ati-mandra̲ saptak.*

1. S̈ means *ṣaḍja̲* of *ati-tār saptak.*
1. G̲̈ means *komal gāndhār* of *ati-tār saptak.*
2. S̤ means *ṣaḍja̲* of *ati-mandra̲-saptak.*
3. M̤̍ means *tīvra̲ madhyam* of *ati-mandra̲ saptak.*

The notes of *ati-mandra̲* and *ati-tār saptak* are rarely used during singing.

Svars of the Indian Musical Scale

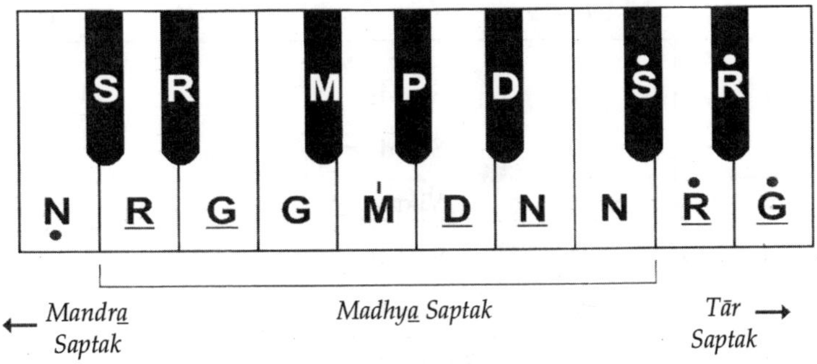


*fig.*: 2.7: Keyboard of Harmonium

Some more information about the notations has been given in 2.18.

## 2.9 Āroh and Avaroh

When the *svars* (in a *rāg*) are arranged in an increasing order of their frequencies, we get what is known as *āroh* and when the order is reversed, the decreasing order is called the *avaroh*. For example, let us consider the *rāg Ahīr-Bhairav,* its *āroh* and *avaroh* are written as

S R̲ G M P D N̲ Ṡ *Āroh*

Ṡ N̲ D P M G R̲ S *Avaroh*

In *rāg Ahīr-Bhairav* all the seven *svars* are used in its *āroh* and *avaroh* so it is a *sampūrṇa̲-sampūrṇa̲*[5] *rāg*. This *rāg* uses *komal r̥ṣabh* and *komal niṣād* (also *komal* or *śuddh madhyam* — see Tables 2.2 and 2.4).

Thus we can summarise that *nād* gives rise to *svars* and *svars* form a *saptak*. In a *saptak* there are seven main *svars*. Out of these "S" and "P" are fixed or *achal* because they are of only one kind, i.e. *śuddh*. Remaining five *svars* have two varieties, namely *śuddh* and *vikr̥t* as shown in the following table.

**Table 2.4**

| *S. No.* | *Tīvra Variety* → | *Known as* ↓ | *Komal Variety* | *Known as* ↓ |
|---|---|---|---|---|
| 1 | R | Śuddh | R̲ | Vikr̥t |
| 2 | G | Śuddh | G̲ | Vikr̥t |
| 3 | M̍ | Vikr̥t | M | Śuddh |
| 4 | D | Śuddh | D̲ | Vikr̥t |
| 5 | N | Śuddh | N̲ | Vikr̥t |

**Note**: Unlike in the case of R, G, D and N, *komal* M is treated as *śuddh* and *tīvra̲* variety is called *vikr̥t* and is represented as M̍.

---

5. Complete.

## 2.10 Thāṭ[6]

*Thāṭ* is a group of *svars* which can be used for making *rāgs*. A *thāṭ* consists of only 7 *svars*, whereas there are 12 *svars* in a *saptak*. Thus a *thāṭ* can be made by choosing any 7 *svars* from the 12 available in a *saptak*. A large number of *thāṭs* can be obtained by permutation and combination of 12 *svars*. But in Hindustani classical music only 10 *thāṭs* have been selected which are considered to be very effective in producing pleasant *rāgs*.

Following are the characteristics of a *thāṭ*

1. Though we have 12 *svars* available for making a *thāṭ*, but out of these we need only 7 for creating a *thāṭ*.

2. The 7 *svars* used to make a *thāṭ* should be written in an ascending order of their frequency such as:

   S, R, G, M, P, D, N. (*Āroh*).

   We know that S and P are fixed or *achal*, but we have 5 *svars* which have two forms, namely *tīvra* and *komal*, any of these can be used for making a *thāṭ* such as:

   S, $\underline{R}$, G, M, P, $\underline{D}$, N.

   or, S, R, $\underline{G}$, M, P, $\underline{D}$, $\underline{N}$.

   or, S, $\underline{R}$, G, M̍, P, $\underline{D}$, N, etc.

3. In a *thāṭ* 7 *svars* are written in an ascending order, such as:

   S R $\underline{G}$ M P D $\underline{N}$

   The *avaroh* is not mentioned because it contains the same *svars* which appear in the *āroh* but put in the reverse order. So the *avaroh* is quite obvious.

---

6. In the word *thāṭ*, the *ṭ* at the end of the word is pronounced like *t* in the English word *lot*.

4. A *thāṭ* does not contain both *śuddh* and *vikr̥t* form of the same *svar.*

5. It is not necessary that the "*svar*-combination" of a *thāṭ* should be always pleasant.

6. To recognise a *thāṭ*, it is generally given the name of a famous *rāg* belonging to that *thāṭ*. For example, *Bhairav* is a very famous *rāg* and so the *thāṭ*, in which it has been kept, has become known as *Bhairav thāṭ*. *Bhairav rāg* is called the *āśraya*[7] *rāg* of the *Bhairav thāṭ*.

### *2.10.1 The process of making 32 thāṭs from 12 Svars*

Consider the octave (*aṣṭak*)

S R G M P D N Ṡ

The 8 *svars* can be divided into two groups

| | | |
|---|---|---|
| *Pūrvāṅg*[8] | S R G M | Group A |
| *Uttarāṅg*[9] | P D N Ṡ | Group B |

In each group 4 kinds of arrangements are possible if we consider both *śuddh* and *komal svars*.

**Table 2.5**

| *Group A* | *Group B* |
|---|---|
| S $\underline{\text{R}}$ $\underline{\text{G}}$ M | P $\underline{\text{D}}$ $\underline{\text{N}}$ Ṡ |
| S $\underline{\text{R}}$ G M | P $\underline{\text{D}}$ N Ṡ |
| S R $\underline{\text{G}}$ M | P D $\underline{\text{N}}$ Ṡ |
| S R G M | P D N Ṡ |

7. Dependent.
8. First half.
9. Second half.

In this way we can have 8 different combinations of 4 *svars* by using *svars* of group A and group B. By mixing the above combinations, we can obtain 16 different combinations of 7 *svars* as shown in Table 2.6.

**Table 2.6**

| | | | | | | | | |
|---|---|---|---|---|---|---|---|---|
| 1. | S | R̲ | G̲ | M | P | D̲ | N̲ | Ṡ |
| 2. | S | R̲ | G̲ | M | P | D̲ | N | Ṡ |
| 3. | S | R̲ | G̲ | M | P | D | N̲ | Ṡ |
| 4. | S | R̲ | G̲ | M | P | D | N | Ṡ |
| 5. | S | R̲ | G | M | P | D̲ | N̲ | Ṡ |
| 6. | S | R̲ | G | M | P | D̲ | N | Ṡ |
| 7. | S | R̲ | G | M | P | D | N̲ | Ṡ |
| 8. | S | R̲ | G | M | P | D | N | Ṡ |
| 9. | S | R | G̲ | M | P | D̲ | N̲ | Ṡ |
| 10. | S | R | G̲ | M | P | D̲ | N | Ṡ |
| 11. | S | R | G̲ | M | P | D | N̲ | Ṡ |
| 12. | S | R | G̲ | M | P | D | N | Ṡ |
| 13. | S | R | G | M | P | D̲ | N̲ | Ṡ |
| 14. | S | R | G | M | P | D̲ | N | Ṡ |
| 15. | S | R | G | M | P | D | N̲ | Ṡ |
| 16. | S | R | G | M | P | D | N | Ṡ |

Note: It appears that each horizontal row contains 8 different *svars* but in fact there are only 7 *svars* because S and Ṡ, both are *ṣaḍja̲*. The only difference is that they belong to different *saptaks*.

In all the 16 variations given in Table 2.6, *śuddh madhyam* has been used. Similarly we can have 16 more combinations by taking *tīvra̱* (or *vikr̥t*) *madhyam*. Thus 32 *thāṭ*s can be prepared from 7 *śuddh* and 5 *vikr̥t svars*. Out of these only 10 *thāṭ*s have been selected for classifying different *rāg*s in Hindustani classical music. Their equivalents in Karnatic music system have been shown in Table 2.7. (Pandit Venkatmakhee was a very eminent musicologist in the south Indian music system who proposed a system of 72 *thāṭ*s.)

**Table 2.7**

| No. | *Thāṭ in Hindustani Classical Music* | *Corresponding thāṭ in Karnatic Music* |
|---|---|---|
| 1 | *Kalyāṇ* | *Mechakalyāṇī* |
| 2 | *Bilāwal* | *Dhīr Śaṅkarābharanaṁ* |
| 3 | *Khamāj* | *Hari Kāmbhojī* |
| 4 | *Bhairav* | *Māyāmālav Gaula* |
| 5 | *Pūrvī* | *Kāmavardhinī* |
| 6 | *Mārwā* | *Gamanasramā* |
| 7 | *Kāfī* | *Kharaharapriyā* |
| 8 | *Āsāwarī* | *Naṭabhairavī* |
| 9 | *Bhairavī* | *Hanumatthoḍī* |
| 10 | *Toḍī* | *Śubha Pantuvarālī* |

The *svars* used in 10 *thāṭ*s in Hindustani music have been given in Table 2.8.

### 2.10.2 Relation between Thāṭ and Rāg

The *rāg* system in Hindustani music is very old and it is not possible to exactly describe when and how it originated and developed into its present form. Some musicologists imagine that perhaps *rāg*s had their origin in folk music which was spontaneous, melodious and provided joy even to common

**Table 2.8**
**Ten Thāṭs used in Hindustani Classical Music**

| *No.* | *Name of the Thāṭ* | *Svars used* |
|---|---|---|
| 1 | *Kalyāṇ* | S R G $\overset{|}{M}$ P D N |
| 2* | *Bilāwal* | S R G M P D N |
| 3 | *Khamāj* | S R G M P D $\underline{N}$ |
| 4 | *Bhairav* | S $\underline{R}$ G M P $\underline{D}$ N |
| 5 | *Pūrvī* | S $\underline{R}$ G $\overset{|}{M}$ P $\underline{D}$ N |
| 6 | *Mārwā* | S $\underline{R}$ G $\overset{|}{M}$ P D N |
| 7 | *Kāfī* | S R $\underline{G}$ M P D $\underline{N}$ |
| 8 | *Āsāwarī* | S R $\underline{G}$ M P $\underline{D}$ $\underline{N}$ |
| 9 | *Bhairavī* | S $\underline{R}$ $\underline{G}$ M P $\underline{D}$ $\underline{N}$ |
| 10 | *Toḍī* | S $\underline{R}$ $\underline{G}$ $\overset{|}{M}$ P $\underline{D}$ N |

* Bilāwal *thāṭ* is regarded as the normal *thāṭ*.

people. The melodic note-combinations in the folk music were then recognised by the music-loving persons who categorised these into different *rāgs*. With the passage of time, the number of *rāgs* kept on growing. Some talented musicians perfected various *rāgs* as a result of their intense practice. In olden times there was a direct transfer of knowledge from the teacher to his students; this tradition continued for a very long time. It is much later that the musicologists wrote treatises on music in which they attempted to provide a theoretical basis to a large number of *rāgs* which were being sung by expert musicians. The very old texts are of only historical value now. In order to understand the present *rāg* system, we shall consider the views of Pandit V.N. Bhatkhande who in the nineteenth-century theoretically systematised the Hindustani classical vocal music. Pandit Bhatkhande attempted to classify different *rāg*s into certain groups of musical notes which are known as *thāṭ*s. Here it is important to note that *thāṭ*s are the mathematical outcome of the permutation and combination of different notes of a *saptak* (see sec. 2.10.1), but *rāg*s meaning colour, joy or passion involve certain unique note-combinations and their presentation in a pleasant manner. In this sense *thāṭ* and *rāg* are conceptually different. The purpose of mentioning the *thāṭ* of a *rāg* is simply to indicate which musical notes are likely to be used in the *rāg* under consideration. The statement that a particular *rāg* has been derived or created from a particular *thāṭ* is in common usage. But strictly speaking, such a statement is not proper. It would be more appropriate to say that a particular *rāg* belongs to, or has been placed in or is based on, a particular *thāṭ*. It should be remembered that *rāg*s existed much earlier whereas the concept of *thāṭ* came only later and is of purely theoretical value.

### 2.11 Varṇa̱

The process of singing consists of *varṇa̱s*: they are of four kinds:

- *Sthāyī Varṇa̱*: Here the same *svar* is repeatedly used such as S, S, S, S; R, R, R, R; G, G, G, G, etc.
- *Ārohī Varṇa̱*: When a singer proceeds from a lower to upper *svar* such as S, G, M, D, N, Ṡ, then it is called *ārohī* style of singing.
- *Avarohī Varṇa̱*: In this style of singing one goes from higher *svars* to lower ones, such as, N, D, M, G; D, M, G; M, G, R; G, R, S, etc.
- *Sañchārī Varṇa̱*: This consists of a mixture of *sthāyī*, *ārohī* and *avarohī* styles of singing, such as, N, D, P; S, S; G, M, D, etc.

The use of all the above *varṇa̱s* is a must for the singing process.

## 2.12 Alaṁkārs

The word *alaṁkār* means ornaments. *Alaṁkārs* are also called *palṭās*. These involve a group of *svars* arranged according to a scheme such as

1. S R G S; R G M R;

   G M P G; M P D M;

2. S R G M; R G M P;

   G M P D; M P D N, etc.

A beginner is asked to practise these *palṭās* regularly so as to attain the capacity to use different *svars* in quick succession. The *palṭās* are used to develop a *rāg* in a stepwise manner.

## 2.13 Rāg

A characteristic composition having beautiful use of *svars* and *varṇa̱s* which sounds melodious and that pleases the audience is called a *rāg*.

Characteristics of a *rāg*:

1. A *rāg* has a base *thāṭ*.
2. It should have a unique combination of *svars* different from the other *rāgs*.
3. A *rāg* should have at least 5 *svars*. The maximum number of *svars* that a *rāg* can have is 7.
4. The *svar* 'S' is always used in a *rāg*, i.e. it is never forbidden.
5. Both, *madhyam* and *pañcham* cannot be simultaneously forbidden in a *rāg*.

6. Normally the two forms (*tīvra* and *komal*) of the same *svar* are not used in a *rāg*, in a way that one follows the other immediately. (There are however, a few exceptions to this rule as in *rāg Lalit*.)

7. A *rāg* should have *āroh* as well as *avaroh* then only it can be completely described. (Difference from *thāṭ*.) For example, let us consider the *āroh* and *avaroh* of the *rāg Paṭdīp*.

   S G̲ M P N Ṡ — *āroh* (5 *svar*s used)

   Ṡ N D P M G̲ R S — *avaroh* (7 *svar*s used)

8. Every *rāg* has a *vādī* and a *saṁvādī svar* which are given more importance during singing that *rāg* as compared to other *svars* of the *rāg*. *Vādī* and *saṁvādī* are used more frequently and singers usually stay for a longer time on these *svars*. *Vivādī svar* is one which should never be used in the *rāg* because it produces an unpleasant effect. However, very efficient singers effectively use this *svar* during the *rāg* and this gives a special pleasure to the listeners. But this is done rarely. Normally there is a gap of three *svar*s between *vādī* and *saṁvādī* of a *rāg*. *Vādī* is regarded as the king, *saṁvādī* as the minister and *vivādī* as an enemy. The other regular *svar*s of the *rāg* are called *anuvādī*. Certain *svar*s are unwanted in a *rāg*; these are called forbidden or *varjit svar*s. For example, let us consider the example of the *rāg Pūriā*.

   *Āroh* : S R̲ G M̍ D N

   *Avaroh* : N D M̍ G R̲ S

In this *rāg*:

*Vādī* is *Gāndhār*

*Saṁvādī* is *Niṣād*

*Varjit* is *Pañcham*

*Anuvādī* are S, $\underline{R}$, $\overset{|}{M}$, D.

9. One of the most important requirements of a *rāg* is that it should be pleasing to ears.

### 2.13.1. *Jāti (Caste) of Rāgs*

We know that *rāg*s belong to different *thāṭ*s. A *thāṭ* always contains 7 *svar*s but this is not compulsory in the case of a *rāg*. A *rāg* can choose any 5, 6 or all the 7 *svar*s from a *thāṭ*. This selection decides the caste or the *jāti* of the *rāg*. There are three major *jāti* of *rāg*s.

1. ***Ouḍav***: Such *rāg*s contain only 5 *svar*s from a *thāṭ* on which they are based. For example, the *rāg Mālkauṅs* uses only 5 *svar*s in its *āroh* and *avaroh* as shown below:

   *Āroh* S $\underline{G}$ M $\underline{D}$ $\underline{N}$ | $\dot{S}$

   *Avaroh* $\dot{S}$ | $\underline{N}$ $\underline{D}$ M $\underline{G}$ S

   This *rāg* has been placed in the *Bhairavī thāṭ*. *Pañcham* and *r̥ṣabh svar*s are forbidden in this *rāg*. *Vādī* of this *rāg* is *madhyam* and *saṁvādī* is *ṣaḍja*.

2. ***Ṣāḍav***: In these *rāg*s one *svar* from a *thāṭ* is forbidden and only 6 *svar*s are used in the *āroh* and *avaroh* of the *rāg*. For example, in the *rāg Pūriā*, 6 *svar*s have been used both in the *āroh* and *avaroh*.

   *Āroh* S $\underline{R}$ G $\overset{|}{M}$ D N | $\dot{S}$

   *Avaroh* $\dot{S}$ | N D $\overset{|}{M}$ G $\underline{R}$ S

*Komal r̥ṣabh* and *tīvra̱ madhyam* are used in this *rāg* which belongs to the *Mārwā thāṭ*. *Pañcham* is forbidden, *vādī* is *gāndhār* and *saṁvādī* is *niṣād*.

3. ***Sampūrṇa̱***: In such *rāgs* all the 7 *svars* of the base *thāṭ* are used in the *āroh* and the *avaroh*. Example is *rāg Bhairav*.

| | | | | | | | | |
|---|---|---|---|---|---|---|---|---|
| *Āroh* | S | R̲ | G | M | P | D̲ | N \| | Ṡ |
| *Avaroh* | Ṡ \| | N | D̲ | P | M | G | R̲ | S |

*Komal r̥ṣabh* and *komal dhaivat* are used (remember *madhyam* is also *komal* but since it is treated as *śuddh*, it has not been underlined). This is a famous *rāg* based on a *thāṭ* which itself is known as *Bhairav thāṭ*. The *vādī* of the *rāg* is *dhaivat* and *saṁvādī* is *r̥ṣabh*.

In the *jātis* of the *rāgs* considered so far, the number of *svars* in the *āroh* and *avaroh* were the same. But this is not always the case. There are several *rāgs* where the number of *svars* in the *āroh* are different from those used in the *avaroh*. Thus from the 3 *jātis*, 6 more *up-jātis* or sub-castes can be produced, so that in all 9 kinds of *jāti* variations are possible as described below.

### 1. Sampūrṇa̱-Sampūrṇa̱

Number of *svars* in *āroh* = 7

Number of *svars* in *avaroh* = 7

**Example**: *Rāg Gauḍ-malhār*: In this *rāg* generally *komal niṣād* is used but the *tīvra̱ niṣād* can also be used along with the *komal* variety. It belongs to the *Khamāj thāṭ*. However, certain authors put it in the *Kāfī thāṭ*.

| | |
|---|---|
| ***Āroh*** | S R G M P D N \| Ṡ |
| ***Avaroh*** | Ṡ \| N̲ D P M G R S |
| ***Vādī*** | *Madhyam* |
| ***Saṁvādī*** | *Ṣaḍja̲* |

**2. Sampūrṇa̲-Ṣāḍav**

Number of *svars* in *āroh* = 7

Number of *svars* in *avaroh* = 6

**Example**: *Rāg Darbārī*

This *rāg* belongs to the *Āsāwarī thāṭ*.

| | |
|---|---|
| ***Āroh*** | S R G̲ M P D̲ N̲ \| Ṡ |
| ***Avaroh*** | Ṡ \| N̲ P M G̲ R S |
| ***Vādī*** | *Ṛṣabh* |
| ***Saṁvādī*** | *Pañcham* |
| ***Forbidden*** | *Dhaivat* in the *avaroh*. |

This one is a serious *rāg* which is sung late in the night (around midnight).

**3. Sampūrṇa̲-Ouḍav**

Number of *svars* in *āroh* = 7

Number of *svars* in *avaroh* = 5

**4. Ṣāḍav-Sampūrṇa̲**

Number of *svars* in *āroh* = 6

Number of *svars* in *avaroh* = 7

**Example**: *Rāg Nanda̲*

Based on *Kalyāṇ thāṭ*.

| | |
|---|---|
| ***Āroh*** | S G M P D N \| Ṡ |
| ***Avaroh*** | Ṡ \| N D P M G R S |
| ***Vādī*** | *Ṣaḍja* |
| ***Saṁvādī*** | *Pañcham* |
| ***Forbidden*** | *Ṛṣabh* in the *āroh*. (Both the *madhyams* are used) |

Sung late in night.

**5. Ṣāḍav-Ṣāḍav**

Number of *svars* in *āroh* = 6

Number of *svars* in *avaroh* = 6

**Example**: *Rāg Janasammohinī*

This has come to Hindustani music from Karnatic music.

| | |
|---|---|
| ***Āroh*** | S R G P D N̲ \| Ṡ |
| ***Avaroh*** | Ṡ \| N̲ D P G R S |
| ***Vādī*** | *Gandhār* |
| ***Saṁvādī*** | *Dhaivat* |
| ***Forbidden*** | *Madhyam* |

Sung in the night.

**6. Ṣāḍav-Ouḍav**

Number of *svars* in *āroh* = 6

Number of *svars* in *avaroh* = 5

**7. Ouḍav-Sampūrṇa**

Number of *svars* in *āroh* = 5

Number of *svars* in *avaroh* = 7

**Example**: *Rāg Paṭdīp*
Belongs to *Kāfī thāṭ*.

| | |
|---|---|
| ***Āroh*** | S G̲ M P N \| Ṡ |
| ***Avaroh*** | Ṡ \| N D P M G̲ R S |
| ***Vādī*** | *Pañcham* |
| ***Saṁvādī*** | *Ṣaḍja* |
| ***Forbidden*** | *Ṛṣabh* and *dhaivat* in the *āroh*. |

**8. Ouḍav-Ṣāḍav**

Number of *svars* in *āroh* = 5

Number of *svars* in *avaroh* = 6

**Example**: *Rāg Rāgeśrī*

Belongs to *Khamāj thāṭ*.

| | |
|---|---|
| ***Āroh*** | S G M D N̲ \| Ṡ |
| ***Avaroh*** | Ṡ \| N̲ D M G R S |
| ***Vādī*** | *Gāndhār* |
| ***Saṁvādī*** | *Niṣād* |
| ***Forbidden*** | *Ṛṣabh* and *pañcham* in the *āroh*, and *pañcham* in the *avaroh*. |

Singing time late night.

**9. Ouḍav-Ouḍav**

Number of *svars* in *āroh* = 5

Number of *svars* in *avaroh* = 5

**Example**: *Rāg Vibhās*
Based on *Bhairav thāṭ*.

| | |
|---|---|
| ***Āroh*** | S $\underline{\text{R}}$ G P $\underline{\text{D}}$ \| Ṡ |
| ***Avaroh*** | Ṡ \| $\underline{\text{D}}$ P G $\underline{\text{R}}$ S |
| ***Vādī*** | *Dhaivat* |
| ***Saṁvādī*** | *R̥ṣabh* |
| ***Forbidden*** | *Madhyam* and *Niṣād*. |

Singing time morning.

Note: In different musical books slight variation in the description of various *rāg*s can be noticed. This should be kept in mind while studying the examples of *rāg*s of different *jāti*s. Musicologists differ on usage of *svar*s in *āroh*s and *avaroh*s of different *rāg*s. There are other types of differences also. For example, certain musicians feel that the *rāg Gauḍ malhār* should belong to the *Kāfī thāṭ* while some put it under *Khamāj thāṭ*.

It has been shown mathematically that from one *thāṭ*, 500 *rāg*s can be created by including all possible *jāti*s hence from 10 *thāṭ*s we can have as many as 5000 *rāg*s. But in practice a much smaller number, say, about 150 or even lesser number of *rāg*s are sung. This is due to the fact that out of so many, only those *rāg*s have been picked up which form a very pleasing combination of notes and can really entertain the audience.

Many *rāg*s have been developed by the refinement of folk tunes (*dhun*) which are very appealing.

### *2.13.2 Rāg-Bhed*[10]

Apart from the classification mentioned in section 2.13.1, the *rāg*s have also been divided into the following three categories.

10. Kinds of *rāg*s.

### 1. *Śuddh rāg*

The *rāg*s which retain their character even when the common *svar*s of other *rāg*s are being used in it are known as *śuddh rāg*s. These *rāg*s are free from the shadow or touch of any other *rāg*. For example, *Bhairav, Toḍī, Kāfī,* etc.

### 2. *Chhāyā-lag rāg*[11]

(i) Sometimes a *rāg* is created by combining two *rāg*s such as *Ahīr-Bhairav* which is a mixture of *rāg Bhairav* and *Kāfī*. In such cases a shadow of one *rāg* on the other is noticeable.

(ii) Sometimes two *rāg*s use more or less common *svar*s in their *āroh* and *avaroh,* but the *svar*s in these *rāg*s are used in different patterns. In such cases, there is a touch of one *rāg* on the other.

(iii) In some instances, two *rāg*s employ the same *svar*s but the *vādī* and *saṁvādī svar*s in the two cases are different: this gives a shadow of one *rāg* on the other.

While singing such *rāg*s one should be careful and should adhere to the rules prescribed for one particular *rāg* otherwise a touch of the second *rāg* will be marked.

Consider the example of *rāg*s *Pūriā, Mārwā* and *Sohnī.* All these *rāg*s belong to the *Mārwā thāṭ* and have common *āroh* and *avaroh* as given below.

*Āroh* : S R̲ G M̍ D N Ṡ

*Avaroh* : Ṡ N D M̍ G R̲ S

Due to the common *svar*s in the three cases, the three *rāg*s become *chhāyā-lag rāg*s. The difference in these three *rāg*s can be understood by considering the following points.

11. Shadow *rāg*.

(a) In ***Mārwā*** : *Vādī* – *Ṛ̥ṣabh*
*Saṁvādī* – *Dhaivat*

"S" is weak in *āroh.* R̲ is used in a particular fashion (called *vakra̱*).

This *rāg* is sung in the evening.

(b) In ***Pūriā*** : *Vādī* – *Gāndhār*
*Saṁvādī* – *Niṣād*

More use of *mandra̱ saptak.*

If R̲ and D are emphasised it will appear to be *Mārwā.* This is a night *rāg.*

(c) In ***Sohnī*** : *Vādī* – *Dhaivat*
*Saṁvādī* – *Gāndhār*

More use of *tār saptak.*

If *mandra̱ saptak* is used, emphasis on R̲ and D will make it similar to *Mārwā*. If G and N are given prominence, the shadow of *rāg Pūriā* will be noted.

### 3. *Saṅkīrṇ rāg*

These *rāgs* are obtained by mixing two or more *rāgs*. Example of this type of *rāg* is *rāg Khat* which is a combination of six *rāgs*. When a *rāg* is created by mixing two or more *rāgs*, then it is called a *miśra̱ rāg.*

### 2.14 Rāg and Time

In the musical literature of Hindustani classical music a particular time is allotted for singing a particular *rāg*. For this purpose 24 hours have been divided into two parts.

1. From 12 noon to 12 midnight.
2. From 12 midnight to 12 noon.

The *rāgs* sung from 12 noon to 12 midnight are called *pūrva̱ rāgs* and those sung from 12 midnight to 12 noon are called *uttar rāgs*.

Consider the "Octave"

S R G M P D N Ṡ

This octave can be divided into 2 parts* as shown below.

| | | | | | |
|---|---|---|---|---|---|
| S | R | G | M | (Part A) | and |
| P | D | N | Ṡ | (Part B) | |

Those *rāgs*, whose *vādī Svar* belongs to part A of the octave, are known as *pūrvāṅgvādī rāgs*; these are in general sung from 12 noon to 12 midnight. The *rāgs* whose *vādī svar* lies in part B of the octave are called *uttarāṅgvādī rāgs*; these are sung from 12 midnight to 12 noon. This is a broad classification and few exceptions to this rule have been observed.

If we consider the time factor, the *rāgs* can be divided into the following three categories.

1. *Rāgs* containing *komal* R and *komal* D (R̲, D̲): these are called *Sandhi-prakāś rāgs*. They have been further divided into two parts:

(a) Morning *Sandhi-Prakāś Rāgs*

These are sung around sunrise (4 a.m. to 7 a.m.). Examples are *Bhairav* and *Kaliṅgarā* — they usually contain *komal madhyam*. Let us consider the *āroh* and *avaroh* of the *rāg Bhairav*:

*Āroh* : S R̲ G M P D̲ N Ṡ

*Avaroh* : Ṡ N D̲ P M G R̲ S

---

* According to certain authors, part A contains notes "SRGMP" and part B consists of "MPDNṠ". However, such a classification creates complications.

This *rāg* is sung in the morning, note that *komal madhyam* has been used in this *rāg*.

(b) Evening *Sandhi-Prakāś Rāgs*

These are sung around sunset (4 p.m. to 7 p.m.). *Rāgs* in this category are *Pūriādhanāśrī* and *Pūrvī*. These contain *tīvra̲ madhyam*. Let us consider the *āroh* and *avaroh* of the *rāg Pūriādhanāśrī:*

*Āroh* : S R̲ G M̍ P D̲ N Ṡ

*Avaroh* : Ṡ N D̲ P M̍ G R̲ S

2. The *rāgs* containing *śuddh* R and *śuddh* D are sung after sunrise and sunset (say 7 a.m. to 10 a.m. or 7 p.m. to 10 p.m.) The evening *rāgs* generally contain *tīvra̲ madhyam*.

Let us take the example of *rāg Bilāwal*

*Āroh* : S R G M P D N Ṡ

*Avaroh* : Ṡ N D P M G R S

This *rāg* is sung between 7 a.m. to 10 a.m. Note that it contains *komal madhyam* and *śuddh r̥ṣabh* and *śuddh dhaivat*.

In the *rāg Kalyāṇ* there are *tīvra̲ madhyam* and *śuddh r̥ṣabh* and *dhaivat*. This *rāg* is sung between 7 p.m. to 10 p.m.

3. *Rāgs* containing *komal* G and *komal* N (G̲ and N̲) are sung during the daytime, say, 10 a.m. to 4 p.m. and in the night 10 p.m. to 4 a.m.

Although the old texts on musicology prescribe different times of the day or night for singing different *rāgs*, in the present times, one cannot strictly adhere to such instructions. These days most of the musical concerts are arranged in the evening, as such singers have to sing various *rāgs* during the first part of the night irrespective of what time has been fixed for those *rāgs*.

## 2.15 Tāl, Mātrā and Laya̱

The term "music" includes singing, playing musical instruments and dance. In all these forms of music the use of *mr̥daṅg* or *tablā* is a must which provides the *tāl*. *Tāl* is a means of measuring time during the performance of music. The *tāl* provided by *tablā* gives the necessary framework of *laya̱* or "speed" around which the different *svars* of the *rāg* are beautifully arranged.

### 2.15.1 *Tāl (Rhythm)*

Particular *svars* are used to frame a *rāg*. Likewise, *bols* are required to make a *tāl*. The common *bols* used in *tablā* playing are Dhā, Dhī, Nā, Tī, Tā, Tirkit, Trik, Tū, Kat, etc. Now let us consider a very simple *tāl* known as Dādrā. It is represented symbolically as

| Dhā | Dhī | Nā | Dhā | Tī | Nā |
|---|---|---|---|---|---|
| X | | | 0 | | |

The above pattern forms one period or *āvartan* of the *dādrā tāl*.

### 2.15.2 *Mātrā*

*Mātrā* means the time-interval between two *bols* of the *tablā*. This time-interval is chosen by the singer and followed by the *tablā* player also. It is this interval which governs the *laya̱* or rhythm of the singing. The *mātrā* or time-interval can have any value such as 0.2, 0.5 or 1 second; the only condition is that it should be fixed for a particular rhythm. One *mātrā* is shown by the sign ◡. It is obvious that one *āvartan* of *dādrā tāl* will have 6 *mātrās*. The *tāl* has been divided into 2 parts or sections by a vertical line. Each part has 3 *bols*. A section or a part is known as *khaṇḍ*.

### 2.15.3 *Laya̲ or Speed or Tempo*

If we keep a time-interval of one second between each *bol* of *dādrā tāl*, one *āvartan* would be complete in 6 seconds. This speed or *laya̲* is generally known as the *madhya̲ laya̲*. If the time-interval between two *bol*s is made more, say, 2 seconds, then 12 seconds will be required for a single *āvartan*. In other words, the speed of playing the *tāl* on the *tablā* will be reduced to half of its original *laya̲;* this is referred to as *vilambit laya̲* (slow speed). The speed of the *tāl* can be further decreased by increasing the time-interval (*mātrā*) between the *bol*s: then we get what is known as *ati-vilambit laya̲*. Only very experienced singers can sing in *ati-vilambit laya̲*.

On the other side of the *madhya̲-laya̲* we have *drut-laya̲*. If the *mātrā*'s time is reduced to ½ second, one *āvartan* of *dādrā tāl* can be reduced to 3 seconds — this is the *drut laya̲*. When the *āvartan* needs only 1.5 seconds for its completion then we get the *ati-drut laya̲*.

### 2.15.4 *Sam*

A cross mark was put below the starting *bol* "Dhā" in the *dādrā tāl*; this denotes the *sam*. The singer as well as the *tablā*-player emphasise this point by giving it prominence and putting it little more forcefully. The *sam* also indicates the beginning of an *āvartan* of a *tāl*. During musical programmes after singing various *svar*s of a *rāg*, the singer and the *tablā*-player simultaneously reach the *sam*; this produces a very pleasing sensation to listeners.

## 2.16 Description of Some Tāls

In the fifteenth century Rājā Mān Singh Tomar of Gwalior promoted the *dhruva-pad* or *dhrupad* style of singing which was very popular in temples and royal courts. *Dhrupad*s were accompanied by *pakhāvaj* or *mṛdaṅg*. Around seventeenth century, *dhrupad* style was replaced by *khayāl* style of singing in which *tablā* was used in place of *mṛdaṅg*. Many *tāl*s have been described which can be played on the *tablā*. Out of these we shall study here only those which are frequently used.

### 1. *Dādrā Tāl (2 parts; 6 mātrās)*

| *Mātrā* | 1 | 2 | 3 | 4 | 5 | 6 |
|---|---|---|---|---|---|---|
| *Bol* | Dhā | Dhī | Nā | Dhā | Tī | Nā |
| *Tāl* symbol | X | | | 0 | | |

The above notation indicates —

(a) There are 2 parts of this *tāl*, each containing 3 *bol*s.

(b) Each *āvartan* is of 6 *mātrās*.

(c) The *sam* in on the first Dhā depicted by a cross written below it.

The first Dhā is therefore played with greater force as compared to the second Dhā. Below the second Dhā, zero appears which denotes *khālī*.

(d) One cycle of basic rhythm with a particular set of *bol*s is called *ṭhekā*.

(e) Part or section means *khaṇḍ* or *vibhāg* in Hindi. (see *fig*. 2.8 on page 60).

We can select the size of the *mātrā* to produce a particular *laya̱* or speed which should match the *laya̱* of the composition sung.

This *tāl* is generally used in *ghaẓal, ṭhumrī, bhajan, gīt,* in folk music and film music.

### 2. *Rūpak Tāl (3 parts; 7 mātrās)*

| *Mātrā* | 1 | 2 | 3 | 4 | 5 | 6 | 7 |
|---|---|---|---|---|---|---|---|
| *Bol* | Tī | Tī | Nā | Dhī | Nā | Dhī | Nā |
| | X | | | 2 | | 3 | |

(a) This *tāl* contains 3 parts and 7 *mātrās*; each *āvartan* is of 7 *mātrās*.

(b) In every case the singing *āvartan* and *tāl āvartan* should match.

This *tāl* is used in *ghazal, gīt, bhajan* and also in classical compositions. The *laya* is played in accordance with the speed of the singing.

### 3. *Keharwā Tāl* (2 parts; 8 *mātrās*)

| *Mātrā* | 1 | 2 | 3 | 4 | 5 | 6 | 7 | 8 |
|---|---|---|---|---|---|---|---|---|
| *Bol* | Dhā | Ge | Na | Ti | Na | Ka | Dhi | Na |
| *Tāl* symbol | X | | | | 0 | | | |

This is a very popular *tāl* in light music just like *dādrā*. It is used in *ghazal, bhajan,* folk music, film music and *gīt.*

### 4. *Jhap Tāl* (4 parts; 10 *mātrās*)

| *Mātrā* | 1 | 2 | 3 | 4 | 5 | 6 | 7 | 8 | 9 | 10 |
|---|---|---|---|---|---|---|---|---|---|---|
| *Bol* | Dhī | Nā | Dhī | Dhī | Nā | Tī | Nā | Dhī | Dhī | Nā |
| Symbol | X | | 2 | | | 0 | | 3 | | |

The cross, zero and the numbers written below the *bols* are helpful in depicting the *tāl* by giving *tālī* (clap).

### 5. *Ek Tāl* (6 parts; 12 *mātrās*)

| *Mātrā* | 1 | 2 | 3 | 4 | 5 | 6 | 7 | 8 | 9 | 10 | 11 | 12 |
|---|---|---|---|---|---|---|---|---|---|---|---|---|
| *Bol* | Dhin | Dhin | Dhā ge | Tir kit | Tū | Nā | Ka | Ttā | Dhā ge | Tir kit | Dhin | Nā |
| Symbol | X | | 0 | | 2 | | 0 | | 3 | | 4 | |

Most of the *khayāls* sung in *vilambit laya* are set to *ek tāl.*

### 6. Tīn Tāl or Tritāl (4 parts; 16 mātrās)

| *Mātrā* | 1 | 2 | 3 | 4 | 5 | 6 | 7 | 8 | 9 | 10 | 11 | 12 | 13 | 14 | 15 | 16 |
|---|---|---|---|---|---|---|---|---|---|---|---|---|---|---|---|---|
| *Bol* | Dhā | Dhin | Dhin | Dhā | Dhā | Dhin | Dhin | Dhā | Dhā | Tin | Tin | Tā | Tā | Dhin | Dhin | Dhā |
| Symbol | X | | | | 2 | | | | 0 | | | | 3 | | | |

This is the most important *tāl* that is used in Hindustani classical music. Most of the *khayāl*s sung in *madhya̱* or *drut laya̱* are set to *tritāl* or *tīn-tāl.*

### 7. Chār Tāl or Chautāl (6 parts; 12 mātrās)

| *Mātrā* | 1 | 2 | 3 | 4 | 5 | 6 | 7 | 8 | 9 | 10 | 11 | 12 |
|---|---|---|---|---|---|---|---|---|---|---|---|---|
| *Bol* | Dhā | Dhā | Dhin | Tā | Kit | Dhā | Dhin | Tā | Tit | Kat | Gadi | Gan |
| Symbol | X | | 0 | | 2 | | 0 | | 3 | | 4 | |

This *tāl* is mainly used during *dhrupad* singing.

Certain *tāl*s like *dīpchandī, jhūmarā* and *tilvāḍā* are also used but rather rarely. *Tāl*s like Brahma̱, Rudra̱, Gaṇeśa̱, Lakṣmī and Viṣṇu are old *tāl*s which are not used during *khayāl gāyakī.*

### 2.17. Madhya̱ Laya̱, Vilambit Laya̱ and Drut Laya̱

Let us now consider an example in which the *laya̱* of the *tablā* has been simultaneously shown, along with that of a song.

The words of the song are — "*Rām Rām Sītā Rām, Rām Rām, Sītā Rām.*" In all there are 8 words in the song.

*Madhya̱ laya̱*: Tīn tāl; 16 *mātrās*; each of one second

| Song | Rā | M | Rā | M | Sī | Tā | Rā | M | Rā | M | Rā | M | Sī | Tā | Rā | M |
|---|---|---|---|---|---|---|---|---|---|---|---|---|---|---|---|---|
| Second | 1 | 2 | 3 | 4 | 5 | 6 | 7 | 8 | 9 | 10 | 11 | 12 | 13 | 14 | 15 | 16 |
| *Bol* on *Tablā* | Dhā | Dhin | Dhin | Dhā | Dhā | Dhin | Dhin | Dhā | Dhā | Tin | Tin | Tā | Tā | Dhin | Dhin | Dhā |
| Symbol | X | | | | 2 | | | | 0 | | | | 3 | | | |

In the above song 16 parts of the song have been sung in 16 seconds for which one *āvartan* of *tīn tāl* is required which is of 16 *mātrās*. This has been regarded as *madhya̱ laya̱*.

Now we will depict the slower speed (*laya̱*) of singing in which each part of the word will be sung in 2 seconds (because here each *mātrā* is of 2 seconds). In this case the singing of the same words will require double the time than that required in the *madhya̱ laya̱* as shown below.

| Song | Rā | ʃ | M | ʃ | Rā | ʃ | M | ʃ | Sī | ʃ | Tā | ʃ | Rā | ʃ | M | ʃ* |
|---|---|---|---|---|---|---|---|---|---|---|---|---|---|---|---|---|
| Second | 1 | 2 | 3 | 4 | 5 | 6 | 7 | 8 | 9 | 10 | 11 | 12 | 13 | 14 | 15 | 16 |
| *Tāl* | Dhā | - | Dhin | - | Dhin | - | Dhā | - | Dhā | - | Dhin | - | Dhin | - | Dhā | - |
| Symbol | X | | | | | | | | 2 | | | | | | | |
| | Rā | ʃ | M | ʃ | Rā | ʃ | M | ʃ | Sī | ʃ | Tā | ʃ | Rā | ʃ | M | ʃ |
| | 17 | 18 | 19 | 20 | 21 | 22 | 23 | 24 | 25 | 26 | 27 | 28 | 29 | 30 | 31 | 32 |
| | Dhā | - | Tin | - | Tin | - | Tā | - | Tā | - | Dhin | - | Dhin | - | Dhā | - |
| | 0 | | | | | | | | 3 | | | | | | | |

This is *vilambit laya̱* which takes 32 seconds for singing the above 8 words whereas the time required for singing these 8 words was only 16 seconds in the *madhya̱ laya̱*. In the *tablā* also now 32 seconds are needed for one *āvartan*.

***Ati-vilambit laya̱*:** If the 16 letters of the above song are sung in 64 seconds, the speed of the *tablā* playing will be further halved and the *āvartan* of *tīn tāl* will now take 64 seconds.

Likewise we can further reduce the *laya̱* of singing.

***Drut laya̱*:** In this *laya̱* the speed of singing and *tablā* playing is faster than that in the *madhya̱ laya̱*. If we complete the singing of 8 words of the song in 8 seconds, the *laya̱* will

* The sign ʃ is called *avagrah*, which means that one should extend the previous note further.

now be double of that in the *madhya laya* — hence this will be known as *duguṇ laya* meaning double speed.

### *Duguṇ laya*

| Song | Rām | Rām | Sītā | Rām | Rām | Rām | Sītā | Rām |
|---|---|---|---|---|---|---|---|---|
| Seconds | 1 | 2 | 3 | 4 | 5 | 6 | 7 | 8 |
| *Tāl* | Dhā Dhin | Dhin Dhā | Dhā Dhin | Dhin Dhā | Dhā Tin | Tin Tā | Tā Dhin | Dhin Dhā |
| Symbol | X | | 2 | | 0 | | 3 | |

The *tablā* speed has also become double so that its *āvartan* now takes only 8 seconds.

### *Chauguṇ laya*

| Song | Rām | Rām | Sītā | Rām | Rām | Rām | Sītā | Rām |
|---|---|---|---|---|---|---|---|---|
| Seconds | 1 | | 2 | | 3 | | 4 | |
| *Tāl* | Dhā Dhin | Dhin Dhā | Dhā Dhin | Dhin Dhā | Dhā Tin | Tin Tā | Tā Dhin | Dhin Dhā |
| Symbol | X | | 2 | | 0 | | 3 | |

Here one *āvartan* will be of 4 seconds. The *laya* of the singing will be four times that of the *madhya-laya*. If one *āvartan* requires only 2 seconds, then the *laya* will become eight times of the original *laya*; this is called *aṭhguṇ laya*.

## 2.18 Some More Information on Notation

1. If the word *Śyām* is written as *Śyām*, it means that this word has to be pronounced in one *mātrā*. It should be remembered that the term *mātrā* represents a fixed interval of time. If the magnitude of the *mātrā* is one second, then *Śyām* will be pronounced in one second.
2. The sign ʃ is called *avagrah* which involves extended utterance of a particular portion of the word of a song. Taking a *mātrā* of one second duration, the

notation *Śyā ʃ ʃ ʃ m* would mean singing the word in 3 *mātrā*s or 3 seconds.

3. A small line – also indicates a *mātrā*. The symbol G – – means that the utterance of the note G is to be extended for two more *mātrā*s.

Some more information on the notation system would be provided in chapter 3.

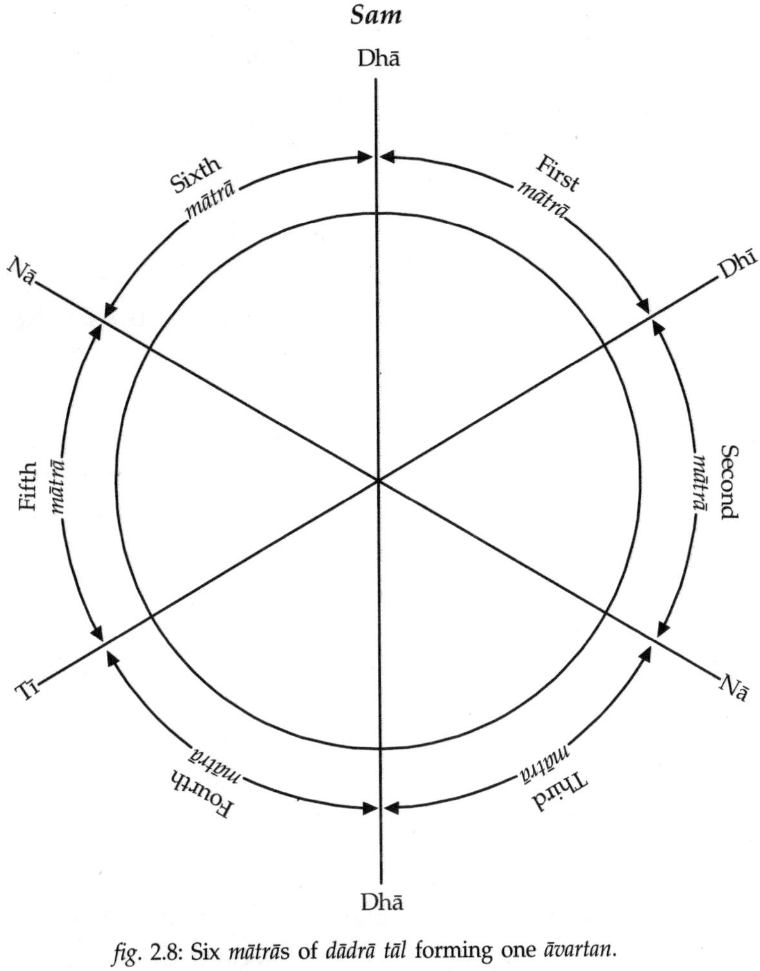


*fig.* 2.8: Six *mātrā*s of *dādrā tāl* forming one *āvartan*.

# 3

# The Singing Process

## 3.1 Mārg (or Mārgī) and Deśī Saṅgīt

In Indian musical literature two categories of music have been described. These are *mārg saṅgīt* and *deśī saṅgīt*. *Mārg saṅgīt* was practised by *gandharva̱s* in very ancient period. The purpose of this music was to please God and attain *mokṣa̱*.[1] It was strictly religious in nature, and was not meant for ordinary masses. Hence it was not known to common people. Later *deśī saṅgīt* was developed by the music *paṇḍits*[2] for public entertainment.

The Indian music has three facets, *gāyan* (singing), *vādan* (playing instruments) and *nṛtya̱* (dance). Out of these, *gāyan* is supposed to be supreme. Human voice is a unique instrument with certain specialities. Firstly, it can function without any external support. Secondly, it has such a timbre that it can produce a large variety of audio effects. Thirdly, words can also be uttered along with singing, thereby inducting a poetic touch to music. In Indian music, the same words are sung in different style, mood and *svars*, thus creating blissful and amazing effect on the audience.

In India, the practice and performance of music is still regarded as religious activity. The *nād* or *svar* is regarded as

1. Salvation.

2. Experts.

equivalent to God. The modern science tells us that sound is simply the outcome of vibrations in material bodies. But the sound or *nād* for creating music involves soul, mind and body — then only, it gives the singer and listeners a supernatural joy and takes them to a different world. The effect of pure *svar*s originating from the soul of a singer has such a tremendous power that the listener is totally lost in the magic of the music. It is believed that the desire to sing originates from one's soul: this sends signal to the mind which activates other organs that produce *svar*s. As a matter of fact when the musical performance reaches its peak, the entire body of the singer and the listeners feel the vibrations. The great singers practise the *svar*s for years, then only their *svar*s produce an effect that cannot be described but only felt at the deepest level of one's heart.

### 3.2 Anibaddh and Nibaddh Gāyan

As per old musical texts, singing has been divided into two categories, namely *anibaddh* and *nibaddh gāyan.*

### 3.3 Anibaddh Gāyan

This type of singing is not bound by *tāl* or rhythm. Here a singer gradually and slowly uses different combinations of *svar*s of a particular *rāg* in such a way as to produce a very pleasant sound effect. This style of singing is called *ālāp.* Normally the practice is that when a singer presents a particular *rāg* in a concert, he starts with the *ālāp* in the *rāg.* This involves a serious and slow singing in which the singer attempts to develop gradually the *svarūp* or picture of the *rāg.* This is necessary because only then he will be able to give out the correct and effective *svar*s required by that *rāg.* This is a very delicate and divine process during which the singer invites the necessary *svar*s. It is the most difficult part of the singing. Once the pure notes start coming out, the necessary mood is created for the singer as well as the audience. A *rāg* generally contains 5, 6, or 7 *svar*s but a talented and experienced singer generates a very large number of different combinations of notes which, although remain in the framework of the *rāg*, appear different from one another and sound very melodious. A gifted and well-trained singer can continue *ālāp* for a considerable length of time without being repetitive.

## 3.4 Nibaddh Gāyan

The singing which is bound by a *tāl* is known as *nibaddh*. An old form of singing style which still exists to some extent is *dhrupad* and *dhamār. Dhrupad* or *dhruvpad*, as the name suggests, consisted of the fixed composition. Later during the sixteenth century, *khayāl* style of singing developed which now constitutes the most important form of singing in Hindustani classical music. In *khayāl* (meaning one's own imagination) singing, although the singer has to restrict himself to only fixed *svar*s prescribed for the *rāg* sung, he has some freedom to use them, in his own way, in order to produce the melody.

*Khayāl gāyakī* consists of *bandiśe*s. A *bandiś* means a song composed using the *svar*s of a *rāg* and following all the rules prescribed for that *rāg*. Normally *bandiśe*s are composed by the great masters of music. The first part of a *bandiś* or a song is called *sthāyī* while the subsequent parts are known as *antarā*s. In *antarā*s, singers normally use notes of higher *saptak*s. The first line of a *bandiś* is called *mukhaḍā*. *Bandiśe*s used in *khayāl* singing are of two kinds.

### *3.4.1 Baḍā Khayāl*

***The bandiśes that are sung at a low speed or laya*****:** Such a *bandiś* is known as *baḍā khayāl*. Most of the *baḍe khayāl*s are accompanied by *tablā* playing *vilambit ek tāl, jhūmrā, tilvāḍā, tīn tāl,* etc. A *baḍā khayāl* starts, after the *ālāp* of the *rāg* has been completed. Although in a *baḍā khayāl* there is restriction of the *tāl,* the *laya̱* is so slow that *ālāp* singing still continues to play a vital part. This is the reason why now singers include the *ālāp* in the *baḍā khayāl* itself. After the *ālāp* of the *baḍā khayāl,* generally *bol-ālāp* is done. This involves pronunciation of the words of the song along with the *ālāp*. The *laya̱* or speed is then slightly increased and *sargam*[3] is included in singing the *rāg*. This is followed by *tān*s both in *ākār*[4] and *sargam*. The lyrics (*bols*) of the *bandiś* are also used in *tān*s which are then known as *bol-tāns*. *Tāns* consist of permutations and combinations of note sequences. Expert singers can perform *tāns* in *duguṇ, chauguṇ* and *aṭhguṇ* (double, four-times and eight-times) speeds. In *aṭhguṇ laya̱* the speed of the singing will be eight times that of the *tāl* played on the *tablā.*

### 3.4.2 Chhoṭā-Khayāl

***The bandiśes that are sung at a faster laya̱:*** After the completion of the *baḍā khayāl,* the usual practice is that another *bandiś* in the same *rāg* is sung in *madhya̱-laya̱* (medium-speed) or *drut-laya̱* (fast speed): this is called *chhoṭā khayāl.*

In *chhoṭā khayāl,* the *ālāp-aṅg* (*ālāp*-part) gradually diminishes and *tāns* become more frequent when singing is done in *madhya̱-laya̱*. The *tāls* used are usually *tīn-tāl, jhap-tāl, rūpak-tāl* or *ek-tāl.* When a *chhoṭā khayāl* is sung in *drut-laya̱,* the *tān-aṅg* (*tān*-part) becomes still more pronounced and it shows the *taiyyārī* (practice) of the singer, as it is quite difficult to render *tān*s in a fast *laya̱*. In this *laya̱,* the *tablā* also plays an effective role. The faster *bandiśes* are generally set to *tīn-tāl* or *ek-tāl.* In such a fast *laya̱,* the *svarūp* of the *rāg* suffers to some extent. However,

3. Utterance of musical notes such as Ni, Dha, Pa, Ga, Re, etc.
4. Singing without using *bol* of the song or *sargam*.

*drut* singing gives a different kind of pleasure as compared to the *ālāp* style of singing.

### 3.4.3 *Tarānā*

After the *chhoṭā khayāl*, some singers present another variety of singing known as *tarānā*. This is sung in *drut* and then in *ati-drut laya̠*. A *tarānā* uses words which have no meaning such as *tāre, dere, nā, tūm, tā, nom, tom, dānī, tādānī, tānānā*, etc. *Tarānās* can be sung in many *rāgs* and are generally set to *ek-tāl* and *tīn-tāl*. The main aim of singing *tarānā* is to demonstrate intense practice (*taiyyārī*), *laya̠kārī* (entertaining the listeners with various patterns of rhythm) and expertise in pronouncing words at a very high speed.

## 3.5 Semi-Classical Music

As has already been mentioned, *dhrupads* have a fixed composition. The *khayāl* type of singing was introduced in order that a singer could take some liberty (within the framework of the *rāg*) and present his own picture of the *rāg*. The sole purpose of *khayāl* singing was to raise the entertainment level. This trend was further extended in the Mughal period when in the royal courts or in private musical concerts entertainment and melody was the prime requirement rather than the purity of the *rāg*. This gave rise to some new styles of singing such as *ṭappā, ṭhumrī, dādrā, ghaẓal, kawwālī*, etc.

### 3.5.1. *Ṭappā*

This is a Hindi word meaning jump, but *ṭappā* is better described as a kind of singing which started from Punjab.[5] It is said that in the *darbār* (royal court) of Āsifudaullā, the king of Lucknow, there was a Punjābī musician called "Shorī Miyāṅ" who invented the *ṭappā* style of singing. It is generally sung in *Kāfī*,

5. A north Indian state.

*Jhiñjhoṭī, Khamāj* and *Bhairavī rāg*s. The words used in *ṭappā*s are mostly Punjābī and Farsi. These contain very typical and complicated *tān*s which demonstrate the *taiyyārī* of the singer. *Ṭappā* singing is of very *chañchal* (non-serious) and swift nature.

### 3.5.2 *Ṭhumrī*

This style of singing was developed in the *rāj-darbār*s of Lucknow. Although *ṭhumrī*s are sung in *rāg*s such as *Pīlū, Bhairavī, Khamāj, Pahāṛī,* etc. more emphasis is on the melody aspect and entertainment of audience rather than on the purity of *rāg*s. *Ṭhumrī*s are set to Punjābī *tīn-tāl* or *dīpchandī* and are sung in *madhya̲ laya̲*. The *ṭhumrī* singers purposely mix other *rāg*s also to create melodious combinations. In the early stages *ṭhumrī* singing was not respected because it ignores the rules of the *rāg*s. But because of its sweetness now almost all the *khayāl* singers conclude their concert with a *ṭhumrī.*

### 3.5.3. *Ghaẓal*

*Ghaẓal*s mostly contain words of Urdu or Farsi. In *ghaẓal gāyakī,* lyrics and tune both are given importance. We can say that *ghaẓal*s are poetry (*ś'er* or couplets) set to tune and sung. *Ghaẓal*s are mostly love-songs set to *dādrā, keharwā, dīpchandī* or *tīn-tāl*. Film music has contributed much in popularising *gīt*s[6] and *ghaẓal*s.

### 3.5.4 *Kawwālī*

In *kawwālī*s also Urdu language is mostly used. The lyrics are composed in praise of God, and these are sung during Muslim festivals in *masjids*[7] or other places. The *kawwālī* singers are known as *kawwāl*s who have a good command over their voice and have a classical touch in their music.

6. Songs (devotional songs are called *bhajans*).
7. Places of worship of Muslims.

### *3.5.5 Dādrā*

These are also mostly love songs similar to *ghazal*s but have a slightly different style. *Dādrā*s are set to *dādrā tāl* and sung in *madhya* and *drut laya*. The *dādrā*s have a touch of folk music.

## 3.6 Light Music

Light music may be broadly defined as any type of singing which is not at all restricted to the framework of any *rāg* or rule. The main constituents of light music can be regarded as *bhajans*, *gīts* and *ghazals*. Although a composer in light music has full liberty to use any note combination, the touch of some *rāg* can invariably be found in the light music. As a matter of fact, most of the composers of light music and film music have a good background of classical music. At times, a *ghazal* or a *gīt* or a *bhajan* may be totally based on *rāg*s. This is the reason why it is difficult to draw a distinct line between light music and semi-classical music. In old film music there was ample use of classical *rāg*s.

During the last 10-20 years, there has been a good deal of inter-mixing in different genres, hence a strict classification of different classes of singing is not possible. For example, now *ghazals* in Hindi are also sung and there are many *kawwālī*s which use Hindi or even Sanskrit words.

## 3.7 Folk Music

Folk music is as old as our civilization. One view is that certain *rāg*s had their origin in the folk music. As an example we can take *rāg Pahāṛī.*

Indian folk music is quite rich and varied. There are very large varieties of songs sung in different regions of India in different seasons and on various occasions. Certain typical folk songs are being briefly mentioned below:

1. *Holī*: This is about *Rādhā-Kr̥ṣṇa̱ Līlā*[8] and is usually sung around *Holī*[9] festival.

2. *Chaitī*: This is also sung during *Holī* and in this style of singing, the lyrics are in praise of "Lord Rām."[10]

3. *Kajrī* or *Kajlī*: Sung during rainy season in the eastern part of Uttar Pradesh.[11]

4. *Nāṭya̱-Saṅgīt*: There is a very rich tradition of *nāṭya̱* or drama in Maharashtra[12] in which music plays a very important role; this type of music is known as *nāṭya̱-saṅgīt*. *Bhajan*s called *abhaṅg*s are also very popular in Maharashtra.

5. *Kīrtan*: *Kīrtan* is normally performed in temples during *pūjā*. Every region has its own style of *kīrtan*. For example, *garbā* in Gujarat.[13]

6. *Boul Saṅgīt* in West Bengal.[14]

7. *Lāvaṇī* in Maharashtra.

Apart from the varieties mentioned above we have a wide range of melodious tunes in the folk music of Punjab,[15] Rajasthan[16] and Maharashtra.

In north India there is a tradition of singing particular types of songs at different religious and social functions.

8. Songs in praise of Hindu god Kr̥ṣṇa.
9. A famous Hindu festival.
10. A Hindu God.
11. A state in northern India.
12. A state in western India.
13. A state in western India.
14. A state in eastern India.
15. A state in northern India.
16. A northern state of India.

There is a vast variety of such kinds of songs. Some of these are mentioned below.

(i) *Ghoḍī, Gārī*: Sung during marriage ceremony.

(ii) *Sohar*: Sung on the occasion of the birth of a child.

(iii) *Māṇḍ*: Sung in Rajasthan. *Rāg Māṇḍ* has been derived from this folk-tune.

### 3.8 Film Music

For the last about 50 years, the contribution of film music in spreading and enriching Hindustani music cannot be undermined. Earlier, the classical musicians did not recognise film music because it did not follow the rules laid down in musical texts. But now it is generally realised that the vast contribution of several talented music directors in the film world have, in a big way, produced awareness in general public towards classical music. Several film songs are based on *rāgs*. Since such songs are sung by common people, the *rāg* unknowingly enters into their mind. Such a feeling creates the capacity in them to appreciate classical music. Kundan Lal Sehgal was a great film singer. Lata Mangeshkar has been awarded *Bhārat Ratna*[17] for her great contribution to film music.

### 3.9 Some Important Musical Terms

Several musical terms have been used so far and their meanings have also been explained as and when required. For the sake of convenience, we shall summarise some of the important ones here.

(i) ***Nād***: Consider, for example, a wire vibrating with a frequency of say 240 oscillations per second. The

17. The highest civilian award given by the Government of India.

sound produced by the wire is a *nād*, note or *svar* (see section 2.3.4 and 2.4).

(ii) ***Śruti***: Any sound that can be heard is *śruti*. But in musical sense, a *nād* which can be distinguished from another one by human ear and which can be used in music is *śruti* (see section 2.5).

(iii) ***Aṣṭak* or *Octave***: The sounds or *nād*s produced by two wires vibrating with frequencies of 240 and 480 respectively form two ends of an "Octave." In between these two end-sounds, music experts have identified 22 *śruti*s (see section 2.10.1).

(iv) ***Saptak***: For practical considerations, 7 *svar*s or notes or sounds have been picked up from 22 *śruti*s. The group of these 7 *svar*s is called a *saptak* (see section 2.6).

(v) ***Śuddh Svar***: After several years of research, the frequencies of these 7 *svar*s have been fixed. These are called *śuddh svar*s. In short form they may be symbolised as:

Sā Re Ga Ma Pa Dha Ni

or

S R G M P D N

(see section 2.6)

(vi) ***Vikṛt Svar***: Apart from 7 *śuddh svar*s, 5 *vikṛt svar*s have also been chosen from 22 *śruti*s; these may be written as

$\underline{R}$ $\underline{G}$ $\overset{1}{M}$ $\underline{D}$ $\underline{N}$

S and P are fixed or *achal*. It means they are of only one variety i.e., *śuddh*. Remaining 5 *svar*s can be either *śuddh* or *vikṛt* (*vikṛt* M is written as $\overset{1}{M}$).

Thus in all we have 12 *svar*s and 22 *śruti*s (see section 2.6).

(vii) ***Mandra, Madhya* and *Tār Saptak*:** The frequency of "S" is taken as 240. The seven *svar*s or notes lie in between frequency range of 240 to 480; these notes are said to be of *madhya-saptak*. The *svar* having the frequency 480, is called *tār* S and is represented by Ṡ. From the *tār* S, another *saptak* starts which is known as *tār-saptak*. The notes on the lower side of frequency 240 will form what is called the *mandra-saptak* (see section 2.7).

(viii) ***Āroh* and *Avaroh*:** When notes are used in an ascending order, they form *āroh* and when used in descending order then we get *avaroh*.

*Āroh* : S R G M P D N

*Avaroh* : N D P M G R S

(see section 2.9)

(ix) ***Rāg*:** A characteristic combination of 5, 6 or 7 *svars* or notes capable of producing melodious singing is called a *rāg* (see section 2.13). The number of *svar*s used in the *āroh* and *avaroh* of a *rāg* may be similar or can be different also. Consider the following example:

**Rāg Śuddh Kalyān**

*Āroh*: S R G P D (5 *svars*)

*Avaroh*: N D P M̍ G R S (7 *svars*)

The *jāti* of the *rāg* is *Ouḍav-Sampūrṇa* (see section 2.13.1).

*Rāg*s can be *Śuddh, Chhāyālag* or *Saṅkīrṇa* (see section 2.13.2).

(x) ***Thāṭ***: It consists of any 7 *svar*s which can be taken from 12 *svar*s available in a *saptak*. All the *rāg*s are derived from *thāṭ*s. *Thāṭ*s have only *āroh*. Although a large number of *thāṭ*s are possible, only 10 are used in Hindustani classical music for the creation of the *rāg*s (see section 2.10).

(xi) ***Anibaddh Gāyan***: Singing without rhythm. This can also be called *ālāp* (see section 3.3).

(xii) ***Nibaddh Gāyan***: Singing with rhythmic accompaniment (see section 3.4).

(xiii) ***Tāl***: It is the means of measuring time during the performance of music. A *tāl* has a fixed number of certain *bol*s (see section 2.15.1).

(xiv) ***Tablā***: A percussion instrument on which *tāl*s are played (see section 6.16).

(xv) ***Mātrā***: The time-interval between two *bol*s of a *tāl*. (see section 2.15.2).

(xvi) ***Laya̲***: Speed or tempo with which a *tāl* is played on the *tablā*, or speed of singing.

*Ati-vilambit laya̲* — Very slow speed
*Vilambit laya̲* — Slow speed
*Madhya̲ laya̲* — Normal speed
*Drut laya̲* — Fast speed
*Ati-drut laya̲* — Very fast speed (see section 2.15.3)

(xvii) ***Dhrupad*** **or** ***Dhruvpad***: An old variety of singing involving fixed compositions (see section 4.2).

(xviii) ***Dhamār***: An old style of singing containing description of *Rādhā-Kr̥ṣṇa Līlā* sung during *Holī* season. The compositions are set to *dhamār tāl* (see section 4.2).

(xix) ***Khayāl-Gāyakī*:** The most popular variety of classical singing in which the singer has a liberty to use the *svar*s in his own way within the framework of a *rāg*. The *khayāl* sung at *vilambit-laya̲* is known as a *baḍā-khayāl* and that at a faster *laya̲* a *chhoṭā-khayāl* (see section 3.4.1 and 3.4.2).

(xx) ***Semi-classical Music*:** *Ṭhumrī, ṭappā* and *dādrā* come under this class of music. Although the base is of a *rāg*, singers mix various *rāg*s to create melody and sweetness and make the singing more entertaining (see section 3.5).

(xxi) ***Bol*:** The words of a song are called *bol*s. A *tāl* is also described by certain words which are also called *bol*s (see section 2.15.1).

(xxii) ***Ālāp*:** Means singing without rhythmic accompaniment (see section 3.3).

(xxiii) ***Sargam*:** Sometimes while singing a *rāg*, the *svar*s or the words of the song are not pronounced. This is known as singing in *ākār*; when *svar*s are uttered during singing it is referred to as singing in *sargam* (see section 3.4.1).

(xxiv) ***Bol-Ālāp*:** Means using the words of the song during *ālāp* (see section 3.4.1).

(xxv) ***Vādī Svar*:** The most prominent *svar* or note of a *rāg* which is more frequently used. Now the "musical octave" can be divided into two parts:

(A) S R G M and

(B) P D N Ṡ

If the *vādī* of a *rāg* lies in the part A of the octave, the *rāg* is said to be *Pūrvāṅg vādī rāg*. These *rāg*s are generally sung in the earlier part of the day, i.e. 12 noon to 12 midnight. If the *vādī* of a *rāg* lies in the part B of the octave, it is known as *Uttarāṅg vādī rāg*. Such *rāg*s are sung in the later part of the day, i.e. 12 midnight to 12 noon (see section 2.14).

(xxvi) ***Saṁvādī Svar***: The second prominent *svar* used in a *rāg*.

(xxvii) ***Anuvādī Svar***: The permitted *svar*s of a *rāg* other than *vādī* and *saṁvādī.*

(xxviii) ***Vivādī Svar***: The *svar*s that are forbidden in a *rāg* (see section 2.13).

(xxix) ***Pakaḍ***: A *rāg* contains a fixed number of *svar*s in its *āroh* and *avaroh.* Out of these *svar*s, smaller groups of *svar*s are identified which are indicative of a particular *rāg*. Such characteristic groups of *svar*s are known as the *pakaḍ* of a *rāg*. When such a group of *svar*s is repeated, the *rāg* is immediately identified by the listeners.

(xxx) ***Lakṣaṇ Gīt***: The music experts have composed songs which very clearly depict the characteristics of different *rāg*s. Such songs are called *lakṣaṇ gīt.*

(xxxi) ***Vakra̱ Svar***: Such a *svar* is not used in a regular or direct manner. In a regular manner *svar*s are pronounced as S R G M, G M P D, P M G R S, etc. Now let us see how N has been used in a *vakra̱* manner in the example, P D N D Ṡ. Here one goes directly from P to N and then returns back to D from N, so the *svar* N will be called the *vakra̱ svar.* Note that R has been used in a *vakra̱* manner in the group of *svar*s, S R S M.

(xxxii) ***Tān***: *Tān* and *ālāp* are the two most important processes of singing. The characteristic *svars* of a *rāg* are pronounced at a very low speed in *ālāp* while in a *tān* this process is done very rapidly (see section 3.4.1).

(xxxiii) ***Bol Tān***: Here the words of the song are uttered during the *tān*. The plain *tān* will be called *tān* in *ākār*. The *svars* can also be pronounced during the *tān;* then it is referred to as *sargam meiṅ tān*. Several types of *tāns* have been described in musical texts.

(xxxiv) ***Mīṇḍ***: When one goes from one *svar* to the other in a continuous manner the process is called *mīṇḍ* in musical language. The symbol $\overset{\frown}{S\ M}$ means that the singer goes from the *svar* S to M in a continuous way in a manner that the in-between *svars* R and G are touched but not heard separately. When the same process is done in a musical instrument, played using a bow, it is called *sūt*.

(xxxv) ***Gamak***: In this process *svars* are vibrated with force generally in *mandra̱-saptak*.

(xxxvi) ***Kaṇ***: While using a *svar* sometimes singers just touch a former or latter *svar* also to make singing melodious. This process can be shown by the symbol. $^{N}\dot{S}$ meaning a touch of *niṣād* is to be given before coming to *tār ṣaḍja̱*. Thus *niṣād* is the *kaṇ svar* and *tār ṣaḍja̱* is the main *svar. Kaṇ svar* can be used after the main *svar* also such as, $G^{M}$, here M is just touched after singing the main *svar* G, i.e. *gāndhār*.

(xxxvii) ***Murkī***: This is also a type of *kaṇ* where three *svars* are used in quick succession such as D M P; the *murkī* is symbolized as $^{DM}P$.

(xxxviii) ***Khaṭkā***: When a *svar* is sung after the previous one with a jerk. This process can involve more than two notes also.

(xxxix) ***Alaṁkār***: It means pronouncing a group of musical notes in different ways using various permutations and combinations. These can be simple or very complicated. The *alaṁkār*s are practised so as to have control over the use of different notes or *svar*s (see section 2.12).

(xl) ***Alpatva̱* and *Bahutva̱***: When in a *rāg*, a *svar* is very rarely used — it is a case of what is known as *alpatva̱*. On the other hand, sometimes a *svar* is used to a greater extent — then it will be a case of *bahutva̱*. Normally *vādī* and *saṁvādī svar*s are more frequently used but in certain cases some other *svar* may also be used prominently.

(xli) ***Tirobhāv* and *Āvirbhāv***: While singing a *rāg*, its rules are observed. But a very important requirement of a *rāg* is that it must sound sweet and melodious. With this object in view even the musical texts permit relaxation in rules to certain extent if this can enhance the sweetness of a *rāg*. For this purpose singers sometimes conceal the *svarūp* (form) of the main *rāg* and permit the shadow of a similar *rāg* to creep in for a short time — this is known as *tirobhāv*. This makes the *rāg* more entertaining. Then they return to the original *rāg* and this is called *āvirbhāv*.

(xlii) ***Parmelpraveśak Rāg***: If two *rāg*s belong to different *thāṭ*s they will create an altogether different atmosphere or mood. This fact causes a problem. When a singer completes a *rāg* of one *thāṭ* and then proceeds to sing another *rāg* belonging to a different *thāṭ*, the effect of the first *rāg* still lingers in his mind which causes difficulty in developing the *svarūp* of the second *rāg*. For example, *rāg Śuddh Kalyāṇ*, containing *śuddh* G and *śuddh* N is sung in the first part of the night. In the second part of the night, *rāg Bāgeśwarī* is sung which contains *komal* G and *komal* N. It is very difficult to switch from a *rāg* containing *śuddh* G and N to another using *komal* G and N. This problem is overcome by singing a *Parmelpraveśak rāg*. *Rāg Jaijaivantī* contains both the *gāndhār*s and both the *niṣād*s (*komal* and *tīvra*). It can be noted that the *svar*s of *Jaijaivantī* are to some extent common to both *Śuddh Kalyāṇ* and *Bāgeśwarī*. Hence, if a singer sings *Jaijaivantī* after *Śuddh kalyāṇ*, he can then smoothly switch to *Bāgeśwarī*. Thus the *rāg Jaijaivantī* in this case will be called *parmelpraveśak rāg*.

# 4

# Gharānās of Music

THE term *gharānā* has been derived from the Hindi word *ghar* meaning house or family. Until the eighteenth century, the Indian music was under the patronage of kings of different states. Every king had a group of talented musicians in his court or *darbār,* who were adequately rewarded. After the eighteenth century the British rule exerted greater pressure on the states. This had an adverse effect on their economic status. The court musicians were therefore forced to have their own schools which later became known as *gharānās:* these played a very important role in keeping the Indian classical music alive for hundreds of years. A *gharānā* consisted of a *guru*[1] and his sons and students who directly received lessons from him. The trained students, in turn, imparted knowledge to their students. In this way a particular style of singing characteristic of the original *guru* continued for hundreds of years and produced a huge following.

A *gharānā* is established by a very talented and devoted singer who, as a result of his practice, discovers some very special and characteristic variety of singing that is not found elsewhere. Gradually, he attracts music lovers and becomes a *paṇḍit* or *ustād.*[2] He then passes on his style of singing to his sons and a few selected students who, he feels, are capable

1. Teacher.
2. Expert.

of keeping alive his style of singing. In olden times the entry of a student into a *gharānā* was quite difficult. One had to render his services to his *guru* for several years before being enrolled into his *gharānā*. Whenever a new student entered the *gharānā* there used to be a public ceremony known as *gaṇḍā-bandhan*. The aspiring student would give gifts to the *guru* who tied a cotton thread called *gaṇḍā* around his wrist. This meant the acceptance of that student into the particular *gharānā*. No artist was recognised unless he belonged to a *gharānā*.

The teaching of music has two aspects:

(a) Theoretical or *śāstra pakṣa*, and

(b) Practical or actual singing known as *gāyakī*.

In earlier times both these aspects were given due consideration. The musical texts were in Sanskrit.[3] Muslims showed interest in Indian music but since they did not know Sanskrit, the theoretical aspect was neglected. Most of the musicians were excellent performers but did not know the underlying theory. During this period, there was greater emphasis on practice which was called *riyāẓ*.

### 4.1 Advantages and Disadvantages of Gharānās

It is a well-accepted fact that knowledge cannot be obtained without a *guru*, hence every musician was related to a *gharānā*. The training in *gharānā*s had advantages as well as disadvantages.

#### *Advantages*

(i) If one was lucky enough to have a really good and honest teacher, the quality of musical training

3. The most prominent language of ancient India.

received by him was of a very high order. For example, Pandit Ravi Shankar was extremely well trained by Ustād Allaudeen Khan, and acquired worldwide fame as a Sitārist.[4]

(ii) Every *gharānā* had a characteristic style which one could not learn from any other source.

(iii) The student had to concentrate only on a particular style of singing, thereby avoiding any confusion or distraction.

***Disadvantages***

(i) In many cases there was a great exploitation of students.

(ii) Many teachers were not up to the mark so obviously students did not get proper lessons. No correction in the training was possible because students were not permitted to have contact with other music teachers.

(iii) Each *gharānā* required a particular voice quality, only then the style of singing could be effective. Sometimes the voice of the student was not so as required by the singing style of the *gharānā*. In such cases the student could not effectively sing and his training became meaningless.

Despite these disadvantages nobody can deny the fact that different *gharānā*s made a significant contribution towards the enhancement of Hindustani classical and semi-classical music. Now, we shall study some of the prominent *gharānā*s of classical singers.

---

4. Expert in playing the musical instrument, *sitār*.

## 4.2 Dhrupad and Vāṇī

Prior to Tānsen there is no reference regarding *gharānā*s but the word *vāṇī* was used to represent a particular style of singing. Akbar ruled the northern India from CE 1556 to 1605. He was a great lover of music. Around CE 1500, Rājā Mān Singh Tomar promoted *dhrupad* style of singing which continued to dominate Hindustani classical music for about 300 to 400 years. In Akbar's court there were four very renowned *dhrupad* singers, namely (i) Tānsen, (ii) Brajchand Brāhmaṇ, (iii) Rājā Samokhan Singh (who was an excellent *vīṇā* player also), and (iv) Śrīchand Rājpūt. In Akbar's time four *vāṇī*s (or styles) were very famous. These were named:

(a) *Gobarhār vāṇī* after Tānsen.

(b) *Khandhār vāṇī* after Rājā Samokhan Singh who was from the place called Khandhār.

(c) *Dāgur vāṇī* after Brajchand who hailed from Dāgur.

(d) *Nohār vāṇī* after Śrīchand who lived in a place called Nohār.

The present *dhrupad-dhamār* style prevailed for about 300 years and then was replaced by *khayāl* singing. Thus there were four schools of *dhrupad* singing, but now *dhrupad* singing has become very rare.

In CE 1500, Sultān Hussain Śirqī developed the *khayāl* style of singing. Around CE 1700, there were two musicians in the court of the Mughal king Muhammad Shāh "Raṅgīle" namely Niyāmat Khān or Sadāraṅg and Feroz Khān or Adāraṅg. They composed a very large number of *khayāl*s in various *rāg*s and practically eliminated the *dhrupad* style of singing. However, it is interesting to note that they themselves used to sing *dhrupad*s and never taught *khayāl* singing to their sons.

There are *gharānās* for dance, for *tablā* playing, for *sitār*, for *ṭhumrī*, etc. also. Here we will consider different *gharānās* of classical singing only.

### 4.3 Delhi Gharānā

This is supposed to be the oldest *gharānā* in *khayāl gāyakī*. The *khayāl* style of singing was popularised by Sadāraṅg and Adāraṅg in the court of Muhammad Shāh Raṅgīle. The last Mughal King, Bahādur Shāh Zafar, was also the patron of *khayāl* singing. His music teacher Miān Achpal (Ghulām Hussain) established "Delhi Gharānā" of *khayāl* singing. Certain people relate this *gharānā* to Sadāraṅg and Adāraṅg. However, most of the musicologists are of the view that after the decline of the Mughal Dynasty, Tānras Khān established the Delhi Gharānā. He had an exceptionally good command over *tāns*. Later, he shifted to Gwalior king Jiyājī Rāo. It is said that the great singers of Paṭiālā Gharānā Alī Bakhsh and Fateh Alī were the students of Tānras Khān. After Tānras Khān, his son, Umrāo Khān, promoted the Delhi Gharānā. Chānd Khān was the last representative of this *gharānā,* which is now almost extinct. In this *gharānā, bandiśes* are very artistic and unique. There is a beautiful use of *bol tāns* in *drut laya̲* demonstrating a good command over *laya̲*.

### 4.4 Gwālior Gharānā

This *gharānā* was established by Natthan Pīrbakhsh whose family tree has been given below:

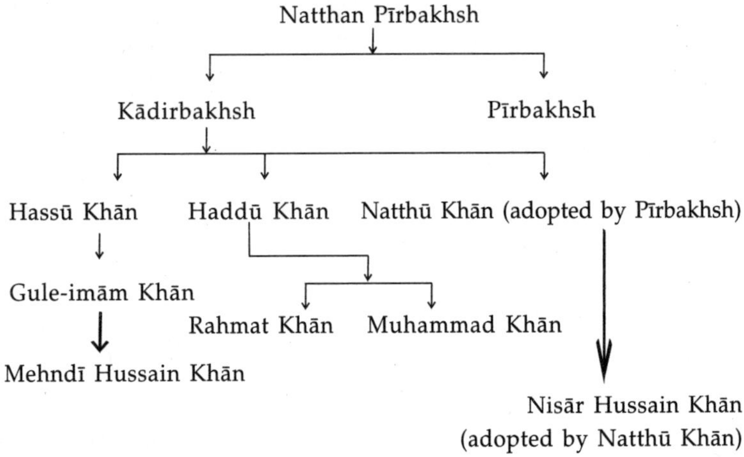


Haddū Khān, Hassū Khān and Natthū Khān were the famous *khayāl* singers in the Gwalior *darbār*. Nisār Hussain Khān was also a very famous singer who trained several well-known singers such as Shankar Paṇḍit, Rām Kṛṣṇa Vaze Buā and Bhāū Rāo. Krishna Rao Pandit and Rājā Bhaiyā Pūñcha Wāle were pupils of Shankar Paṇḍit.

Following are the characteristics of the Gwālior Gharānā:

(i) Forceful and open-throated voice (*buland, khulī āwāẓ*)

(ii) *Dhrupad* touch in *khayāl* singing.

(iii) *Sīdhī* and *sapāṭ tāns*.

(iv) Use of *gamak* in *tāns*.

(v) *Layakārī* in *bol tāns*.

#### 4.5 Āgrā Gharānā

One view is that this *gharānā* was started by Alakhdās and Malūkdās. Some believe that Tānsen's son-in-law Hājī Sujān Khān initiated this *gharānā*. Later Khudābakhsh Ghagghe made it popular. There are many similarities between Āgrā and Gwālior Gharānās because Khudābakhsh had learnt *khayāl gāyakī* from Natthan Pīrbakhsh of Gwalior. Faiāz Khān was a very famous singer who earned a great name for Āgrā Gharānā, The family tree of Āgrā Gharānā is given below.

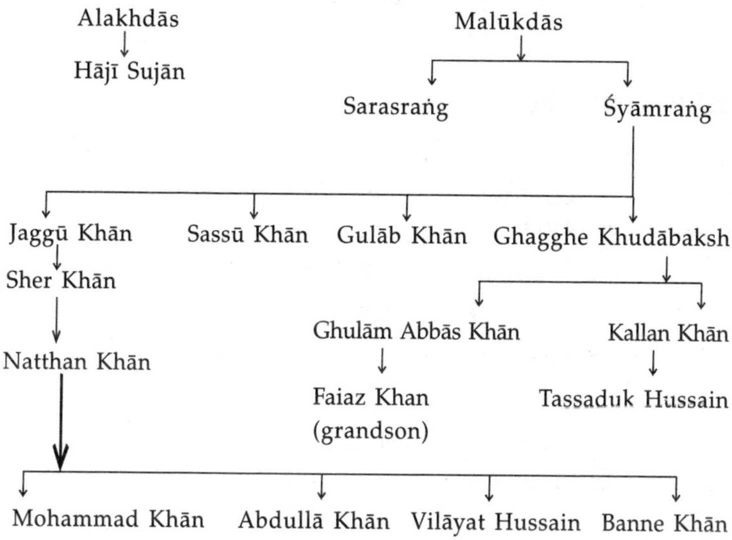


### *Characteristics of Āgrā Gharānā*

(i) *Ālāp* in *dhrupad* style using the words *nom-tom* during singing.

(ii) Forceful or open throat *gāyakī* (*khulī-buland āwāẓ*)

(iii) Good preparation in *bol-tāns*.

### 4.6 Jaipur Gharānā

Manraṅg is supposed to be the founder of this *gharānā*. Muhammad Alī (from the family of Manraṅg) further developed this *gharānā*. His son Āśik Alī Khān also used to sing but later took to *sitār* playing. This *gharānā* then got split into two *gharānās*, namely Paṭiālā Gharānā and Allādiā Khān's Gharānā.

The singing style of this *gharānā* was characterised by small *bandiśes*, *vakra tāns*, open throat voice (*khulī āwāẓ*) and beautiful style of using notes. Aliyā and Fattū, and Allādiā Khān of Jaipur Gharānā started two separate *gharānās*.

### 4.7 Paṭiālā or Punjab Gharānā

This *gharānā* has become very famous due to Ustad Bade Ghulam Ali Khan who was one of the greatest *ṭhumrī* singers. During 1857 there was great chaos in Delhi so most of the Delhi singers moved to Paṭiālā. In those days the states were very rich and their kings used to be great patrons of fine arts. Paṭiālā was one of the best known states in Punjab.

Tānras Khān of Delhi was in Paṭiālā *darbār*. His two students Alībakhsh and Fateh Alī were very famous. In their singing there was a beautiful combination of *gāyakī* of Delhi, Gwalior and Jaipur Gharānās. Both were known as "Aliyā-Fattū." The son of Alībakhsh, Bade Ghulam Ali Khan was one of the Punjābī artists who earned great fame for the Paṭiālā Gharānā. He had many talented students like his son Munawar Ali Khan, Prasoon Banarjee and famous *ghaẓal* singer from Pakistan Ghulam Ali. Bade Ghulam Ali took lessons from his uncle Kale Khan first in *sāraṅgī* and then in singing. Salamat Ali and Nazakat Ali were also very talented and famous for their singing in *drut-laya* and very melodious *ṭhumrīs*. Prior to the Partition of India they were in Paṭiālā *darbār* but later shifted to Pakistan. Both the brothers sang together (*jugalbandī*). It is said that there was a touch of magic in their music.

Special features of Paṭiālā Gharānā are:

1. Melody and beautiful *harkat* and *murkiyā͟n* (special way of using notes).
2. Complicated *tān*s and very fluent use of notes.
3. Artistic *bandiś*es. Skillful *tān*s even in very fast speed.
4. Bade Ghulam Ali Khan knew *sāraṅgī* playing also: this inducted great melody and the art of *mīṇḍ* in his *gāyakī.*

The family tree of Paṭiālā Gharānā is as follows:

- Bābā Kālidās
  - Baharām Khān
    - Kālū Khān
      - Alībakhsh
      - Fateh Alī
        - Āśik Alī
        - Kāle Khān
        - Alī Bakhsh (Kasurwāle)
          - Ghulam Ali
            - Munawar Ali
          - Barkat Ali
          - Mubarak Ali
          - Aman Ali

### 4.8 Kirānā Gharānā

This *gharānā* has a special place in Hindustani classical music. It is said that once a village was totally destroyed due to flood in the river Yamunā. The natives of the village were given land by the king Jahāṅgīr in a place called Kirānā. These people had great interest in music. Later they accepted Islam and a *gharānā* came up which was known as Kirānā Gharānā. This was supposed to be initiated by Sādik Alī Khān who was a famous *bīnkār* (*vīṇā* player). His son Bande

Ali Khan was also a *bīnkār* and used to sing as well. He then became the court musician in Indore state. His main students were Murād Khān (*bīnkār*) and Nanhe Khān (*dhrupad* singer). Later Abdul Karim Khan and Abdul Wahid Khan were the most prominent singers of this *gharānā*. This *gharānā* was very popular in Maharashtra. Several famous singers such as Savāī Gandharva, Suresh Babu Mane, Heerabai Barodekar, Bhimsen Joshi, Saraswati Rane, Gangubai Hangal, Ustad Amir Khan, Rajjab Ali Khan, etc. belonged to the Kirānā Gharānā.

The salient features of Kirānā *gāyakī* are:

1. Special style of projecting a note.
2. More importance to *svars* as compared to the lyrics.
3. Gradual development (*upaj* or *baḍhat*) of a *rāg*.
4. *Ālāp*-oriented singing.
5. A touch of *ṭhumrī* style (*aṅg*).
6. Good use of *mīṇḍ* and *gamak*.

There are certain other *gharānās* of *khayāl* singing also such as Allādiā Khān's Gharānā, Atrolī Gharānā, Sahaswān Gharānā, Śyām Chaurāsī Gharānā, etc. Due to the movement of the artists from one place to another, there has been some inter-mixing of styles of different *gharānās*.

### 4.9 Present Status of Gharānās

These days music teaching has become more liberal. Now there are several means available for listening to many eminent singers. There are regular musical concerts in the different parts of the country. Moreover, records, tapes, CDs are freely available. The upcoming singers have now all the facilities for assimilating the good points of several singers.

For this reason, *gharānās* are no longer of any great importance now. In Hindustani classical music there is a great deal of freedom to the singer to present his imagination within the framework of a *rāg*. Although even today a singer would mention his *gharānā* and his teacher's name he uses only basics of that *gharānā* and creates the *rāg* melody in his own way.

# 5

# Some Eminent Musicologists and Singers of Hindustani Classical Music

FROM the present-day status of Hindustani classical music, it is not difficult to conclude that its evolution and development up to the present level must have taken several thousand years and contribution of a very large number of dedicated musicians. Even if we consider the period of the last about 500 years, we can identify a pretty long list of very talented singers, dancers and instrumentalists. As such it is not possible to give their life histories in a monograph of this type. However, the contribution of some of the well-known singers and authors of musical texts will be briefly described here.

## 5.1 Bharat

He wrote the book *Nāṭyaśāstra̲*. It is supposed to be the oldest musical text which was prepared sometime between 200 BCE and CE 200. Although the subject matter of this book pertains to drama or *nāṭya̲*, it also contains information about various musical instruments and other aspects of music.

## 5.2 Mataṅga̲

The musical treatise *Bṛhaddeśī* was written by Mataṅga̲ in the eighth century. It includes many topics discussed in *Nāṭyaśāstra*. By this time several *rāgs* were framed which were quite popular. This book gives a detailed account of the *rāgs* and their classification.

### 5.3 Nārad

Nārad's *Saṅgīt Makarand* was created in the eighth century. This book also deals with the classification of various *rāgs*. An attempt has been made to relate *rāgs* with *ras* (mood). Perhaps there was some other author also having the same name who wrote the book *Nāradiya Śikṣā*.

### 5.4 Jaidev

He is known for his famous book *Gīt Govind* written in the twelfth century. This book has been translated not only in different Indian languages but also in Latin, German and English. Apart from being an excellent poet, he had a good knowledge of music. This is obvious from the fact that for each of his poem, the *rāg* and *tāl* have also been mentioned. In many temples his poems are recited with music and dance.

### 5.5 Śāraṅgdev

He was the court musician of Devgiri (later known as Daulatābād) during the thirteenth century. He is acclaimed as a great musicologist because of his book *Saṅgīt Ratnākar* which is treated as the basic text by the musicians of Hindustani as well as Karnatic music. The book deals with all the three departments of music, namely singing, instrument playing and dancing. A very large number of *rāgs* have also been described. It appears that the *rāg saṅgīt* at the time of Śāraṅgdev had undergone an enormous change as compared to that at the time of Bharat and Mataṅga. Many new *rāgs* had come up. From this point of view *Saṅgīt Ratnākar* can be regarded as a novel treatise on music.

Apart from the above-mentioned books, there were other important books also written by Hindustani as well as Karnatic musicians. Some of these have been named below:

| Treatise | Period (century) | Author |
|---|---|---|
| *Rāgataraṅginī* | Fourteenth | Lochan |
| *Rāgamālā* | Sixteenth | Puṇḍrīk Viṭṭhal |
| *Swarmel Kalānidhi* | Sixteenth | Rāmāmātya |
| *Mānkutuhal* | Sixteenth | Mān Singh Tomar |
| *Saṅgīt Darpaṇ* | Seventeenth | Dāmodar |
| *Chaturdaṇḍī Prakāśikā* | Seventeenth | Veṅkaṭamakhī |
| *Saṅgīt Pārijāt* | Seventeenth | Ahobal |
| *Rāg-tattva Vibodh* | Eighteenth | Śrīnivās |
| *Saṅgīt Sār* | Eighteenth | Sawaī Pratāp Singh |
| *Nagmāte Āsfī* | Nineteenth | Muhammad Raẓā |
| *Saṅgīt-rāg Kalpdrum* | Nineteenth | Kṛṣṇānand Vyās |

After considering certain important books on music, now the contribution of a few great singers is briefly mentioned.

### 5.6 Swāmī[1] Haridās

Swāmī Haridās enjoys the same status in Hindustani classical music as Tulsīdās in the field of religious literature. The date and the place of his birth are controversial. However, from different available sources it can be inferred that he was born in western Uttar Pradesh in the later half of the fifteenth century. From the early childhood he was inclined towards music. At the age of 25 he shifted to Vrindāvan and started

1. Saint.

living like a sage in a small hut. Certain musical texts describe him as a "Nād Brahma-Yogī."[2] He had a number of students who earned great fame, Tānsen being the most famous one. The descendants of Tānsen headed the different *gharānā*s of singers and *vīṇā* players (*bīnkār*s). As such, Swāmījī through Tānsen, can be credited for establishing a big network of class musicians throughout the northern part of India.

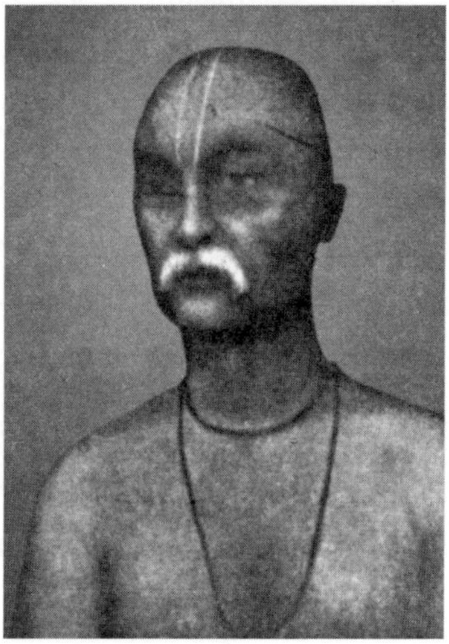

It is said that once King Akbar told Tānsen that he wanted to listen to his *guru*'s music. Since Swāmījī never came out of Vrindāvan, Akbar and Tānsen went to him and requested him to sing. But Swāmījī did not agree. Then Tānsen himself started singing and knowingly made a mistake. At this point Swāmījī could not resist himself and correctly sang the composition in order to point out the mistake to his pupil Tānsen. Swāmījī's singing was so effective and divine that Akbar was amazed and asked Tānsen as to why he couldn't sing like his *guru*. Tānsen then explained to Akbar that while

2. A saint totally dedicated to music.

he sang to please kings, his *guru*'s music was to please God, this made his music so effective.

**5.7 Tānsen**

In India *saṅgīt* has one more name and that is Tānsen. Around CE 1500, there lived a brāhmaṇa in Gwalior known as Makarand Pandey or Miśrājī. It is said that a *sūfī* (saint) Mohammad Gaus, gave him *duā* (boon) that he will be blessed with a son who will earn great fame. The son of Makarand was named Tannā. This boy was an expert in producing different kinds of sounds. One day when Swāmī Haridās was passing through the village, he heard the roar of a lion. On searching, it was found that the lion's roar was produced by Tannā. Swāmījī was impressed by the boy and took him to Vrindāvan where Tannā learnt music for about 10 years and became famous as "Tānsen." At the time of his father's death he came to Gwalior. His father asked him to go to Mohammad Gaus and instructed Tānsen never to disobey the saint. At Gwalior, Tānsen lived with Mohammad Gaus and also taught music to the queen of Gwalior, Mṛganayanī. She got him married to her maid — Hussainī. Tānsen had

four sons — Surat Sen, Śarat Sen, Taraṅg Sen and Bilās Khān. He also had a daughter called Sarasvatī. All of them turned out to be good musicians. After the death of Mohammad Gaus, Tānsen was with the king of Rewa for some time and ultimately went to Delhi to become the chief musician in Akbar's *darbār*. He was a great favourite of Akbar and by this time was regarded as the topmost singer of the country. He created many new *rāg*s such as *Miyāṅ kī Toḍī, Miyāṅ Malhār*, etc. His son Bilās Khān propagated the tradition of his father. Tānsen's daughter was married to Miśrī Singh who was an excellent *bīnkār*. Later on he was known as Naubat Khān; he headed a *gharānā*. Most of the singers and *vīṇā* players thus originated from Tānsen's family.

### 5.8 Gopāl Nāyak

Gopāl Nāyak was the court singer in Deogiri in the thirteenth century. When Alauddīn Khiljī attacked Deogiri he brought with him a famous musician Amīr Khusro. It is said that there was a competition in which by using some trick Amīr Khusro defeated Gopāl Nāyak. But Khusro as a matter of fact knew that Gopāl Nāyak was an extraordinary singer, so he took him to Delhi. Gopāl Nāyak had a special place amongst his contemporaries.

### 5.9 Amīr Khusro

The father of Amīr Khusro was Mohammad Saifuddīn who came to India from Balban and settled in Etah district. Some authors say that Amīr Khusro was born in CE 1234 while according to certain others he was born in CE 1253 in the village Paṭiālī of Etah district in Uttar Pradesh. Amīr Khusro is regarded as a very intelligent person and a versatile artist. He has a long list of achievements to his credit in the field of music and literature. He served in the courts of many Muslim

rulers. It is said that he designed *tablā* and *sitār* — the two most important musical instruments. According to some authors he invented the *Chhoṭā khayāl gāyakī, tarānā* and *kawwālī* style of singing. He is supposed to have discovered new *rāg*s such as *Pūriyā, Sājgiri, Sarpardā* and *tāl* like *jhūmrā* for playing on the *tablā*. He was the author of some musical texts and a very well-known folk poet. However, certain authors regard that such a huge contribution is beyond the capacity of a single person.

### 5.10 Sadāraṅg and Adāraṅg

In the eighteenth century there was a very famous *bīnkār* (*vīṇā* player) and singer called Niyāmat Khān, in the court of the Mughal king Mohammad Shāh. Niyāmat Khān was a descendant of the daughter of Tānsen. Niyāmat Khān was also known as Sadāraṅg. Although earlier Amīr Khusro, Sultān Hussain Śirqī and others had attempted to develop *khayāl* singing they could not make it popular. It was Sadāraṅg who composed a very large number of *khayāl*s and incorporated the name of the king in the lyrics. This idea worked and the *khayāl gāyakī* was accepted by public. In many of Sadāraṅg's *khayāl*s, the words *sadāraṅgīle momadsā* have been used. According to some historians Niyāmat Khān had two sons, Feroz Khān or Adāraṅg and Bhūpat Khān or Mahāraṅg. In many *khayāl*s the word Adāraṅg also appears. In any case Sadāraṅg and Adāraṅg will always be remembered as far as *khayāl gāyakī* is concerned.

### 5.11 Haddū Khān

Haddū Khān and his brother Hassū Khān were very gifted and famous singers of the Gwalior Gharānā. They were grandsons of Natthan Pīr Bakhsh, the founder of the Gwalior Gharānā. Haddū and Hassū Khān were great favourites of Jiyājī Rāo, the king of Gwalior. It is said that at that time there was no singer of the like of Haddū Khān in India.

### 5.12 Hassū Khān

Hassū Khān and his brother Haddū Khān belonged to Lucknow. Their father Kādirbakhsh died when they were quite young. For security reasons their grandfather Natthan Pīr Bakhsh took them to Gwalior. At that time the king of Gwalior Daulat Rāo Shinde was a great patron of music. He gave shelter and all support to Natthan Pīr Bakhsh who established the Gwalior Gharānā.

Hassū Khān was a talented singer with wonderful voice which was a gift of God, while Haddū Khān had done lot of practice to train his voice. Both the brothers were considered to be the topmost singers of India.

### 5.13 Faiaz Khan

He was born in 1886 in a village Sikandarā near Agra. Because of the death of his father he learnt singing from his maternal grandfather Ghulām Abbās Khān. Later he also got music lessons from his relatives Natthan Khān and Fidā Hussain of Kota in Rajasthan. Then he went to Mysore for some time and eventually became the court singer of Baroda state in Gujarat.

He was one of the finest *dhrupad* and *khayāl* singers of his time. His *gharānā* was known as Raṅgīlā Gharānā. He had a bold but sweet voice and had a very impressive personality. He also recorded his music for gramophone companies. Some of his well-known students were Dilip Chand Bedi, Azmat Hussain, S.N. Ratanjankar, etc.

**5.14 Bade Ghulam Ali Khan**

He was born in 1902 in Lahore. His father Alībakhsh and uncle Kāle Khān were famous singers. He had four brothers

who were also good musicians. In the earlier part of his training he learnt playing *sāraṅgī* (a very sweet musical instrument which can produce sound close to human voice). It was his expertise in *sāraṅgī* which imparted extra sweetness to his singing. He was a *ṭhumrī* singer *par excellence* besides being a *khayāl* singer. He was the illustrious musician of Punjābī Gharānā.

### 5.15 Amir Khan

He was the son of Shahmir Khan, the court singer of Indore state. He received training in music from his father for 25 years. His intensive training and dedication to music made him one of the greatest masters of *khayāl* singing. He would sing effortlessly in *ati-vilambit laya̲* which had immense effect on his audience. He also sang for certain films. The touch of his singing is evident in his main student Amarnāth. It was most unfortunate that this great artist died untimely in a road accident.

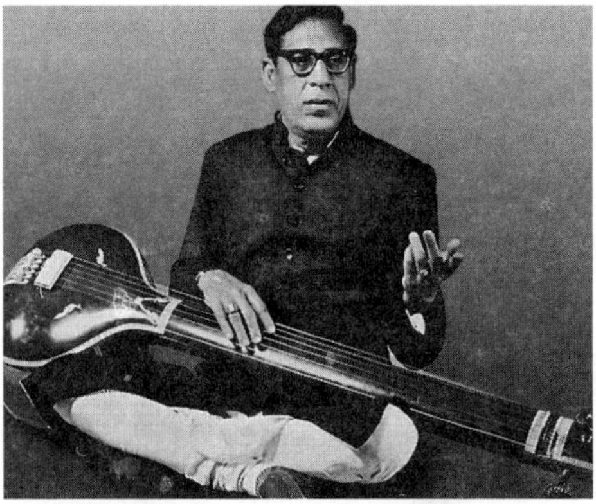

### 5.16 Abdul Karim Khan

He is the most famous singer of Kirānā Gharānā. This *gharānā* has produced several excellent singers and instrumentalists. Abdul Karim Khan got training in music from his father Kāle Khān and uncle Abdullā Khān. He became an efficient singer from very early age. At the age of 15 years he was invited by the ruler of Baroda as his court singer. From Baroda he went to Bombay and finally settled at Miraz (Maharashtra).

In 1913 he established Arya Sangeet Vidyalaya in Pune. He is known for his melodious singing. Gramophone records of his songs and *ṭhumrīs* are available. He had several students who later earned a great deal of fame; among them were Heera Bai Barodekar, Sawai Gandharva, Roshanara Begum, etc.

**5.17 Kumar Gandharva**

He was born in 1924 in Belgaum district. He got encouragement from his father who arranged for his music

training. He was a natural singer and had a characteristic style of singing. He was attached to Sangeet Vidyalaya established by Prof. Deodhar at Bombay. Due to illness he left Bombay and shifted to a small but peaceful place called Dewas situated in Madhya Pradesh (a state in central India).

### 5.18 Vishnu Narayan Bhatkhande

He was born in Bombay in 1860. He was a law graduate but was more inclined towards music. He is mainly responsible for the spread of Indian classical music throughout the country in the twentieth century (see section 1.14).

### 5.19 Vishnu Digambar Paluskar

He was born in 1872 in Belgaum. He along with Bhatkhande played a pioneer role in promoting the Indian classical music (see section 1.14).

### 5.20 Omkarnath Thakur

He was born in 1897 in a village near Baroda. He was the main student of Paluskar. In 1917 he became the principal of "Gandharva Mahavidyalaya" Lahore. He gave musical concerts not only in India but also in several European countries. Apart from being a good performer he was an excellent teacher. He was the Head of the Music Department of Banaras Hindu University.

There are several other singers also who had significant contribution in the development of Indian classical music in the twentieth century. Some of the most famous vocal singers have been mentioned below:

Alladia Khan, Abdul Wahid Khan, Mushtak Hussain Khan, Maula Bakhsh, Mallikarjun Mansur, Vinayak Rao Patwardhan, D.V. Paluskar, Krishna Rao Pandit, Jasraj, Jitendra Abisheki, Bhimsen Joshi, Rashid Khan, Gangubai Hangal, Heera Bai Barodekar, Kesar Bai Kelkar, Prabha Atre, Girja Devi, Kishori Amonkar and Parvin Sultana.

In the field of instrumental music also, in the last century a tremendous progress has been made so much so that now there are several music schools of Indian classical music in Europe and America.

# 6

# Some Musical Instruments

INDIAN music has three basic forms, namely singing (*gāyan*), playing instruments (*vādan*) and dance (*nr̥tya̱*). Archaeological excavations at Mohen̐jo-Daṛo and Haṛappā provide evidence about the existence of musical instruments (*vādya̱s*) during Indus-Valley Civilization around 2500 BCE. Mention has been made of musical instruments such as *vaṅśī, vīṇā, mr̥daṅg, bherī, dundubhi, ḍamrū*, etc. in *Rāmāyaṇ* and *Mahābhārat*. Thus from various historical sources it can be concluded that musical instruments were in use as far back as 5000 BCE or even earlier.

## 6.1 Classification of Indian Musical Instruments (Vādya̱s)[1]

The Indian musical instruments can be broadly classified into the following four categories:

(a) *Tat*
(b) *Avanaddh*
(c) *Suṣir*
(d) *Ghan*

## 6.2 Tat Vādya̱

The instruments containing strings of metals or of some other material such as guts are known as *tat vādya̱s*. These are

1. Plural of *vādya̱* (musical instrument).

played either by finger nails or by using a striking device, made of some hard material, called *mizrāb* (plectrum). Some of the examples of *tat vādya̲s* are *vīṇā, sitār, sarod, surbahār, santūr, svarmaṇḍal, tānpūrā*, etc.

There is another variety of *tat vādya̲s* called *vitat*, in which a bow (*gaẓ*) is used in place of a *mizrāb*. The friction between the bow and the strings produces sound, as in violin, *sāraṅgī, isrāj*, etc. Western musical instruments such as mandolin, guitar and violin belong to the category of *tat vādya̲*.

### 6.3 Avanaddh Vādya̲

These instruments consist of hollow structures, of various shapes and sizes, made of metal, wood or mud. The upper open part of the structure is covered with the skin of some animal (parchment). When this cover is struck with a stick or hand, different types of sounds are produced depending upon the nature of the skin and shape and size of the hollow body of the instrument. *Avanaddh vādya̲s* are invariably used along with singing or other musical instruments in all kinds of music world over. Examples of *avanaddh vādya̲s* are *pakhāvaj, mr̥daṅg, tablā, ḍholak, ḍamrū*, etc. *Ḍamrū* is said to be the favourite of Lord Śiva̲. Drums and, octopad are also *avanaddh vādya̲s* which are used in Western music.

### 6.4 Suṣir Vādya̲

In these instruments, air is used to produce sound. *Vaṅśī* (flute) is the most famous example of *suṣir-vādya̲*. Lord Kr̥ṣṇa was the greatest *vaṅśī* player. Harmonium is the most common and a frequently used instrument in which air is blown in to produce sound. Clarinet, trumpet, accordion, and mouth organ too are *suṣir vādya̲s* which are now being used in India also, especially in film music.

### 6.5 Ghan Vādya

In these instruments sound is produced by striking metal plates or pieces of wood or metallic tubes or rods of different sizes. In an instrument called *jal-taraṅg*, pots of different sizes made of China clay are used. These pots are filled with suitable amounts of water so that different *svar*s are produced when the pots are struck with wooden sticks. Piano is also an example of *ghan vādya*.

During the last about 50 years there has been greater interaction between Western and Indian music. As a result, several Western instruments such as clarinet, trumpet, mandolin, saxophone, xylophone, piano, guitar, mouth organ, violin, accordion, etc. are often used in Indian music while Indian instruments like *tablā* and *sitār* are sometimes included in the orchestra of Western music.

Some of the important musical instruments used in Indian music have been described here.

### 6.6 Vīṇā

This is an ancient musical instrument. Some people call it *bīn*. At present *vīṇā* is more popular in south India. In olden times *vīṇā* was an important instrument in north India, but these days it is used very rarely. Two types of *vīṇā*s are used in India, one in the north and another in the south. The *vīṇā*s used in the north are called *brahma vīṇā* and *rudra vīṇā*. The *vīṇā* of the south is known as *tañjore vīṇā* or *sarasvatī vīṇā*. There is a very rich tradition of *vīṇā-vādan* in south India where this art is very much respected.

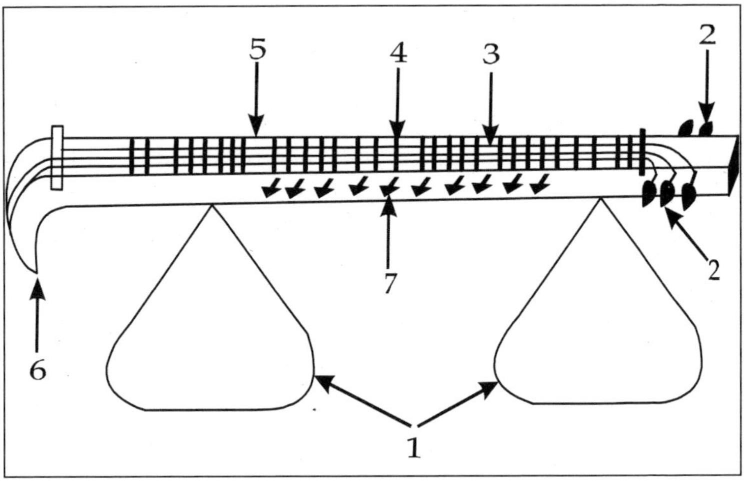


*fig*. 6.1: *Vīṇā* (Diagrammatic)

Different components of a *vīṇā* are as under:

1. *Tūmbā* (gourd — made of dry hollowed pumpkin).
2. Tuning pegs (rotatable wooden knobs for adjusting the tension of main strings).
3. Main strings.
4. Frets or *pardā*s.
5. *Daṇḍ* (a piece of hollowed seasoned wood about 3½ ft long and 3 inches in width).
6. A small peg of ivory or wood to tie the strings.
7. Smaller pegs for tuning sympathetic or secondary strings called *tarab*s. About 20 such *tarab*s are placed beneath the main strings in a parallel direction (the *tarab*s have not been shown in the figure, only their pegs are visible).

In old musical texts several types of *vīṇā*s have been described which differ in size, shape and number of strings used. The strings are made of different metals. Certain parts of body of animals (guts) are also used as strings; these are used to produce *svar*s of *mandra̱* and *ati-mandra̱ saptak*s.

The *vīṇā*s can be divided into two types:

(i) *Śruti-vīṇā*

(ii) *Svar-vīṇā*

The purpose of *śruti-vīṇā* is to give out certain fixed *svar*s which are common to those used by a singer. These *svar*s provide musical background to the singing, thus making it more pleasant. *Tānpūrā* is an example of *śruti-vīṇā* which every vocal musician uses during singing. Another example of this type of instrument is *svar-maṇḍal*. *Śruti-vīṇā* is not used as a solo instrument.

*Svar-vīṇā* is used as an accompaniment to the singing. Here, a *vīṇā* player produces various *svar*s to match those used by a singer. *Svar-vīṇā* is also used in solo playing.

### 6.6.1 The Structure of Vīṇā

*Vīṇā* consists of a thick hollow piece of wood (or bamboo) which is about 3.5 ft in length and 3 inches in width; this is called *daṇḍ*. At the two ends of the *daṇḍ*, two hollow spheres (made from dry pumpkin) are attached which act as sound boxes; these are called *tumbā*s (gourds). On the upper surface of *daṇḍ*, there are vertical partitions called *pardā*s (frets) or *sārikā*s which could be of wood or brass. In some *vīṇā*s these *pardā*s are fixed and in some they are movable. The strings are made of metals and also of intestines of certain animals (guts). Strings are fixed at one end of the *daṇḍ* and attached to knobs at the other end. By rotating the knobs (pegs) in clockwise or anti-clockwise directions the strings can be given the desired tension needed to produce a particular *svar*. By pressing the string at different *pardā*s different *svar*s can be heard (see *fig*. 6.1).

During the Jain and Bauddh period, several types of *vīṇā*s were already developed. Śāraṅgdev has mentioned some of them in his musical treatise, as given below.

### 6.6.2 *Different Types of Vīṇā*s

(i) ***Ek*[2]*-Tantrī*[3]**: This is also known as *ghoṣikā*. It contains only one string hence it is also called *ek-tārā*. It is played with a striker (*miẓrāb*) made of a piece of bamboo. By pressing the string (which is normally made of intestine of an animal) by the fingers of the right hand at different places, different *svar*s can be produced. This is said to be the *ādi*[4] *vīṇā* which was later on developed into other kinds of *vīṇā*s.

(ii) ***Tri*[5]*-Tantrī***: It contains a *daṇḍ* made of a bamboo piece on which there are 14 *pardā*s. As is clear from the name it contains 3 strings. Later on it was improved upon by using 16 *pardā*s and 6 strings. It is also known as *kinnarī*.

(iii) ***Chitrā***: Its basic structure is similar to *kinnarī*. The only difference is that it contains 7 strings, which is why it is known as *sapt*[6]*-tantrī* also.

(iv) ***Vipañchī***: It contains 9 strings and hence is also known as *nav*[7]*-tantrī*.

(v) ***Mattakokilā***: It contains 21 strings. It is said that the celestial sage Devarṣi Nārad used to play this *vīṇā*.

---

2. *Ek* in Hindi means one.
3. String.
4. Ancient.
5. *Tri* in Hindi means three.
6. *Sapt* means seven.
7. *Nav* means nine.

Apart from the above kinds there are several other types of *vīṇā*s also which use 1 to 100 strings and have different shapes. In many *vīṇā*s supporting strings (called *tarab*s) are also used which make the sound of a *svar* richer and sweeter.

In Akbar's court Rājā Samokhan Singh was a very renowned *vīṇā* player. His descendants kept alive his tradition or *gharānā* which produced excellent *vīṇā* players or *bīnkār*s. Bande Ali Khan and Swami Parvatikar are famous *vīṇā* players of Hindustani music.

## 6.7 Tānpūrā or Tambūrā

This is one of the most important instruments in Indian classical music. It is not used to play *alaṁkār* or *rāg* but provides a rich musical background to vocal or instrumental artist. Vocal musicians always use *tānpūrā* as a base instrument during a performance. *Tānpūrā* can also be called *śruti-vīṇā*. In ancient times *ek-tantrī vīṇā* was used as an accompaniment while singing. Gradually, this was more and more refined and it has taken the form of present-day *tānpūrā*. These days electronic *tānpūrā*s are also available but the traditional *tānpūrā* has retained its importance due to its deep resonant sound which forms a perfect base for the human voice.

### *6.7.1 The Structure of Tānpūrā*

This is made of about 4 ft long hollow piece of wood called *daṇḍ*. Its upper surface is almost flat and is about 3 inches in width. The lower part of the *daṇḍ* is attached to a big *tūmbā* made of hollow dried pumpkin (see *fig*. 6.2).

The upper part of the *daṇḍ* has 4 knobs to control the 4 strings used in the *tānpūrā*. These 4 strings are tied to the bottom of the *tūmbā*. Normally the first 3 strings are of steel and the fourth one is that of brass. The *tānpūrā* does not contain *pardā*s. The first string is tuned to the *pañcham svar* of the *mandra saptak,* second and third strings (known as *joḍī ke tār*) to the *ṣaḍja* of the *madhya saptak* and the fourth one to the *ṣaḍja* of the *mandra saptak.* On plucking these four wires one by one slowly and softly by the fingers of the right hand, a musical atmosphere is created that provides a very sweet background to the vocal recital.

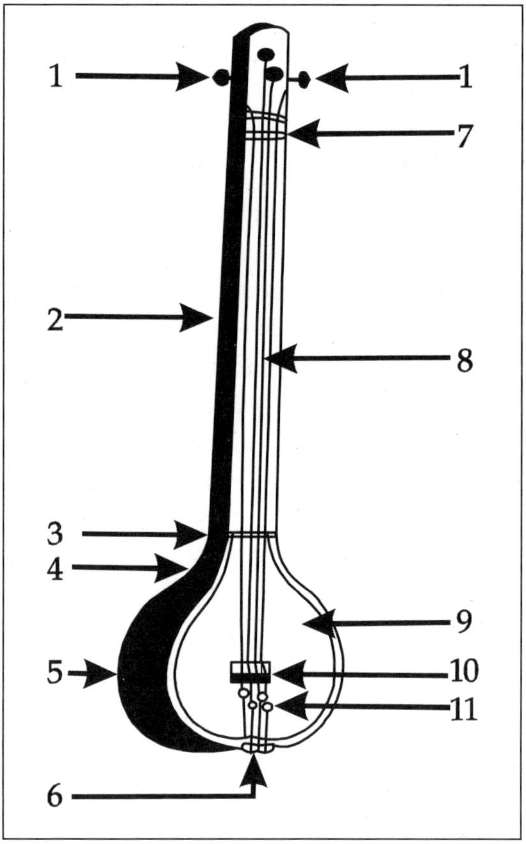


*fig.* 6.2: *Tānpūrā*

Different parts of a *tānpūrā* are as under:

1. Pegs for tuning strings.
2. *Daṇḍ.*

3. *Gul* — the junction of *tūmbā* and *daṇḍ*.
4. Some decorative design.
5. *Tūmbā* (gourd — dry hollowed pumpkin).
6. Nail for tying strings.
7. *Aṭī* — a plastic or ivory plate on which strings rest.
8. Strings.
9. *Tablī* — upper wooden cover of *tūmbā*.
10. Bridge.
11. Plastic balls for fine tuning of strings.

### 6.8 Svar-Maṇḍal

Like *tānpūrā*, this is also used as a supporting instrument for singing. It consists of a triangular hollow structure made of

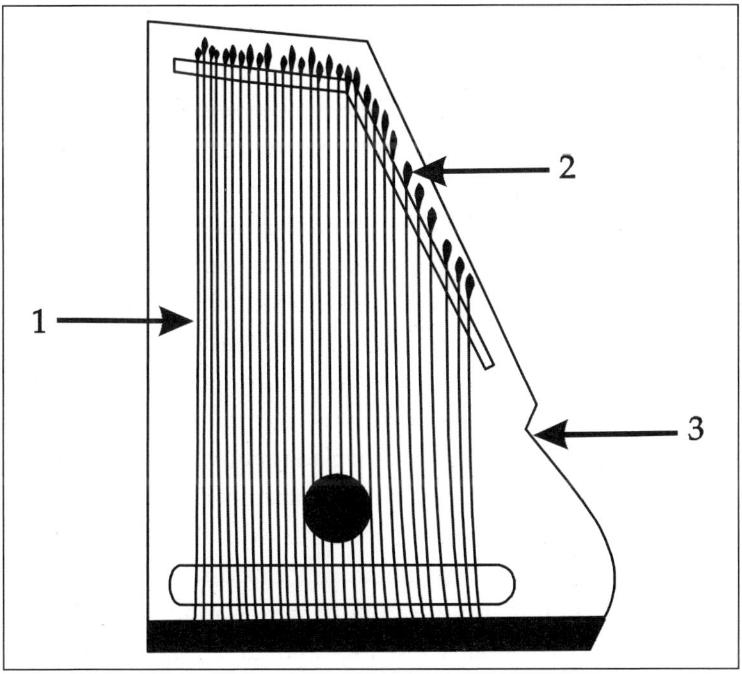


*fig.* 6.3: *Svar-maṇḍal* (Diagrammatic)

wood. At the upper surface there are about 30 metallic strings of various thicknesses. Due to the triangular shape of the instrument, strings have varying lengths. Knobs are also provided to adjust the tension of the strings so that they can be tuned to different *svar*s used in the *rāg* being performed. The strings are occasionally plucked softly by finger nails in quick succession. This creates a very pleasant atmosphere while singing (see *fig* 6.3).

Different components of a *svar-maṇḍal* are as under:

1. Strings.
2. Knobs for tuning the strings.
3. Hollow structure (sound box).

### 6.9 Sitār

At present *sitār* is the most widely used string instrument in north India. There are various views regarding its origin. One view is that it was developed by modifying the ancient *tri-tantrī vīṇā.* Another view is that it was designed in the thirteenth century by Amīr Khusro who was the court musician of Alauddīn Khiljī. However, no reference of this instrument is found in the musical texts until the eighteenth century. There is one more theory about the origin of *sitār.* In the earlier part of the eighteenth century there was a very famous musician known as Sadāraṅg in the court of Mohammad Shāh Raṅgīle who was a great music lover. It is said that the younger brother of Sadāraṅg was Khusro Khān who used to play many *rāg*s on an instrument having 3 strings. Many musicologists believe that this was the beginning of *sitār.* At that time this instrument was called *seh-tār* (*seh* means 3 in Persian language). Gradually it was modified and the present-day *sitār* contains 7 strings and 23 *pardā*s (see *fig*. 6.4).

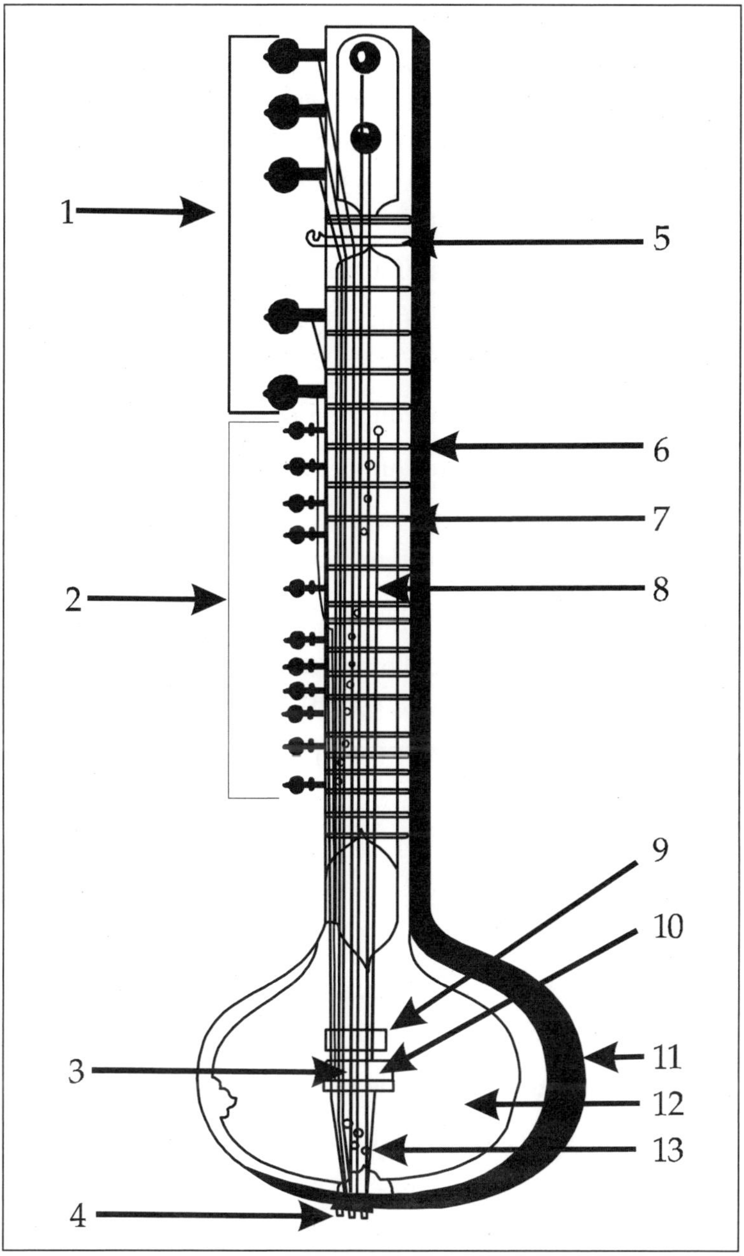


*fig.* 6.4: *Sitār* (Diagrammatic)

Whatever may be the truth about the origin of *sitār,* today it is regarded as a perfect and a very melodious instrument. There have been several excellent *sitār* players in the last about 100 years who have beautifully explored all the possibilities of this instrument. Like in vocal music, there are different *gharānā*s of *sitār* players also.

Different components of a *sitār* are as under:

1. Tuning pegs for adjusting the tension of the main strings.
2. Smaller pegs for tuning the *tarab*s.
3. Main strings (7 in number made of steel, brass and copper wires).
4. A small peg of ivory or plastic to tie the strings.
5. Plastic or ivory bridge on which main strings rest.
6. *Daṇḍ* (a piece of hollowed, seasoned wood about 3 ft long and 3 inches in width).
7. *Pardā*s (frets made of brass).
8. *Tarab*s (secondary or sympathetic strings of thin steel wire). About 15 such strings are placed beneath the main strings. Only one *tarab* (see no. 8) has been shown in *fig*. 6.4.
9. Small bridge over which *tarab*s are stretched.
10. Main bridge over which main strings are stretched.
11. *Tūmbā* (gourd — made of dry hollowed pumpkin).
12. *Tablī* (upper wooden cover of *tūmbā*).
13. *Mankā*s (plastic or ivory balls) for fine tuning of main strings.

### 6.9.1 *The structure of Sitār*

The basic components and the structure of *sitār* are very much like *vīṇā.* As a matter of fact, *sitār* is a modified form of *vīṇā.* The main part of the instrument is about 3 ft long piece of wood which is hollow; this is known as *daṇḍ.* The width of *daṇḍ* is about 3 inches and its upper surface is slightly depressed so as to accommodate the supporting strings called *tarab*s. The lower part of the *daṇḍ* is joined to a *tūmbā* which is made of dried, hollow pumpkin. In certain *sitār,* a small *tūmbā* is attached to the upper part of the *daṇḍ* also to improve the tonal quality of the instrument. There are 19 to 23 *pardā*s (made of brass) which are tied to the *daṇḍ* at different positions. Seven strings are used in *sitār*: their ends are tied to the lower part of the *tūmbā.* The other ends of the strings are attached to 7 rotable knobs situated at the upper part of the *daṇḍ.* There are 11 smaller wooden knobs in the middle portion of the *daṇḍ* to which supporting strings or *tarab*s are attached. The *tarab*s are tuned (with the help of the knobs) to the *svar*s being used in the *rāg* that is played on the *sitār.* The first main string is called *bāj kā tār.* When it is plucked with a metallic conical striker called *miẓrāb,* a note is produced. Different *svar*s can be obtained by pressing the main string by the index or middle finger of the left hand at different *pardā*s. The *mizrāb* is worn on the index finger of the right hand. By striking the *bāj kā tār* with *miẓrāb, bol*s like Dā, Rā, Dir, are produced. When a *svar* is produced on the main wire the corresponding *tarab* also vibrates, thereby producing resonance which not only enhances the intensity of the *svar* but also makes it sound very pleasant.

There are different *gharānā*s of *sitār* associated with very eminent artists. Two types of *bandiśe*s are played on *sitār. Masīt khānī gat* was developed by Maseet Khan which is played at a slow speed. The other type of *gat*[8] was developed by Raza Khan which is played at a faster speed and is known as *raẓā khānī gat*. In the last 50 years there have been a number of *sitār* players who have made this instrument very popular not only in India but also in other countries. Some of the eminent *sitār* players are Ravi Shankar, Vilayat Khan, Nikhil Banarji, Abdul Halim Jafar, Balram Pathak, Imdad Khan, Inayat Khan, Rais Khan and Shujat Khan. Ms Annapurna and Imrat Khan played *surbahār*, an instrument very much similar to *sitār*.

### 6.10 Santūr

This is an old musical instrument from Kashmir.[9] It is said that this is the revised form of the ancient *ṣaṭ-tantrī-vīṇā* which contained 100 strings. It has a hollow triangular structure which acts as a sound box. The top surface of the structure

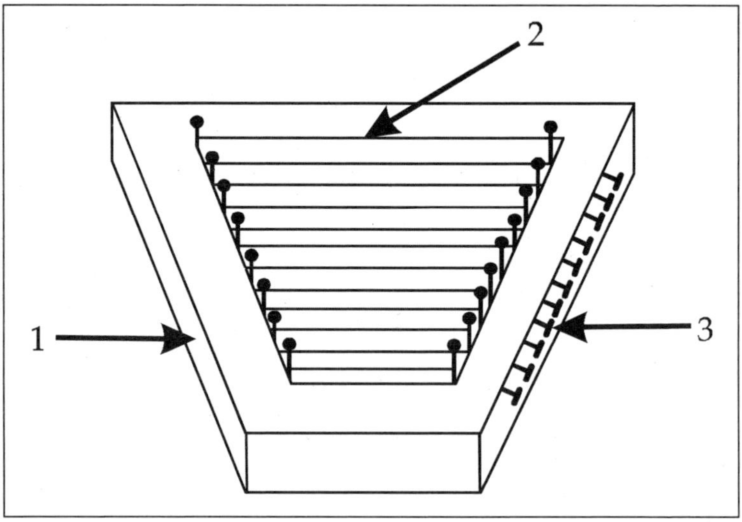


*fig*. 6.5: *Santūr* (Diagrammatic)

8. Composition played on a musical instrument.
9. Northern part of India.

contains a number of strings of varying lengths. The tension of these strings can be adjusted with the help of knobs to which these strings are attached. Different strings are tuned to the different *svar*s of the *rāg* being played. The instrument is played by striking the strings with two wooden sticks using both the hands (see *fig*. 6.5). Shiv Kumar Sharma has played a significant role in promoting this instrument. This instrument can also be treated as a *ghan vādya̲*.

Different components of a *santūr* are as under:

1. Hollow wooden structure (sound box).
2. Strings.
3. Knobs for tuning the strings.

### 6.11 Sarod

This instrument came to India with the advent of Muslim rulers. It is smaller in length than *sitār.* It has a somewhat cylindrical sound box to which a *daṇḍ* is fixed. It does not contain *pardā*s. The strings can be tuned to proper *svar*s with the help of adjusting knobs. In this instrument the wires are thicker, hence its sound is different from that produced by the *sitār.* The strings are struck by a small piece of some hard material using the right hand. The front part of the *daṇḍ* is flat (without *pardā*) on which strings are pressed by the fingers of the left hand to produce different *svar*s (see *fig*. 6.6). Allaudin Khan, Ali Akbar Khan, Hafiz Ali Khan, Sharan Rani, Zarin Daruwala and Amjad Ali Khan are some of the noted *sarod* players.

Different components of a *sarod* are as under:

1. Upper *tūmbā*.
2. Pegs for tuning the main strings.
3. Plate on which main strings rest.

4. Smaller pegs for tuning *tarabs*; there are about 15 *tarabs* which are placed beneath the main strings in parallel direction (*tarab*s have not been completely shown in the figure).
5. *Tarab*s (only partly shown).
6. Small bridge on which *tarab*s rest.

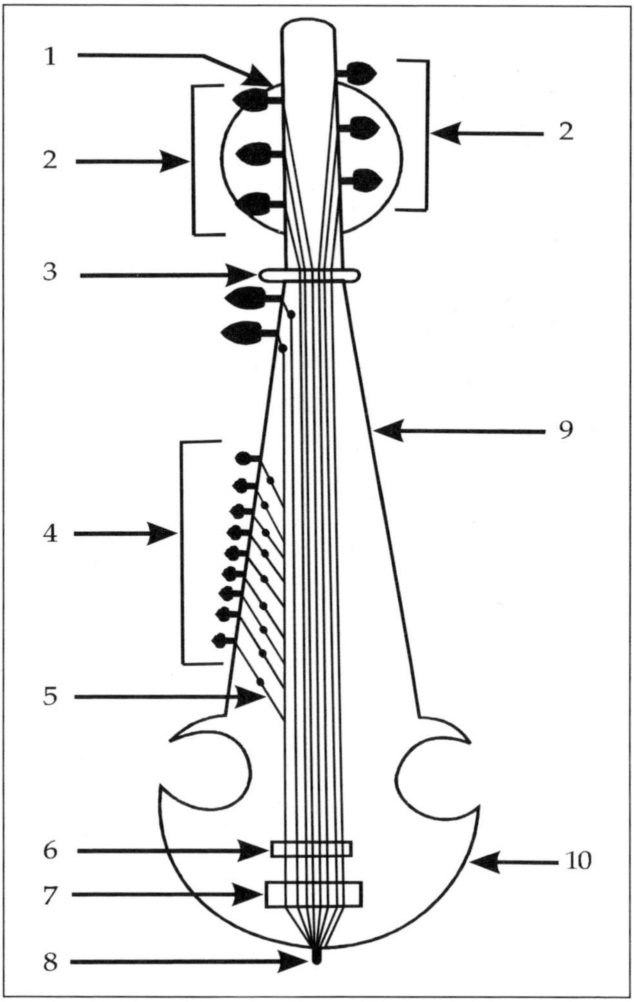


*fig.* 6.6: *Sarod* (Diagrammatic)

7. Main bridge on which main strings are stretched.
8. A peg for tying strings.
9. *Daṇḍ.*
10. *Tūmba* whose upper part is covered with parchment.

So far we have considered those string instruments in which sound is produced by plucking the strings with a striker. There is another class of string instruments in which sound is produced as a result of friction between the strings and a bow or *gaẓ:* such instruments are called *vitat vādya̱*. The bow consists of hair of some animal or threads of some synthetic material. The most important instruments belonging to this class are violin, *sāraṅgī* and *isrāj*.

### 6.12 Violin

This is a foreign instrument which has been adopted by Indian musicians both in the north and south India. Violin is used in Indian classical music as well as in light music.

Different components of a violin are as under:

| | |
|---|---|
| 1. Peg Box, | 12. Finger Board, |
| 2. Neck, | 13. Nut, |
| 3. Strings, | 14. Peg, |
| 4. F Hole, | 15. Scroll, |
| 5. Chinrest, | 16. Frog, |
| 6. End Pin, | 17. Eyelet, |
| 7. Tailpiece, | 18. Hair, |
| 8. E Tuner, | 19. Tip, |
| 9. Bridge, | 20. Stick, |
| 10. Sound Post (inside), | 21. Bow Grip, |
| 11. Ribs, | 22. End Screw. |

### *6.12.1 The Structure of Violin*

The body of violin consists of a flat hollow structure made of wood which is the sound box. About 1 ft long and 2 inches wide piece of wood is attached to the body of the instrument. This flat plate is called the finger board. Normally 4 strings of different thicknesses are used in violin. These strings are tied to the lower part of the body. The strings are then set

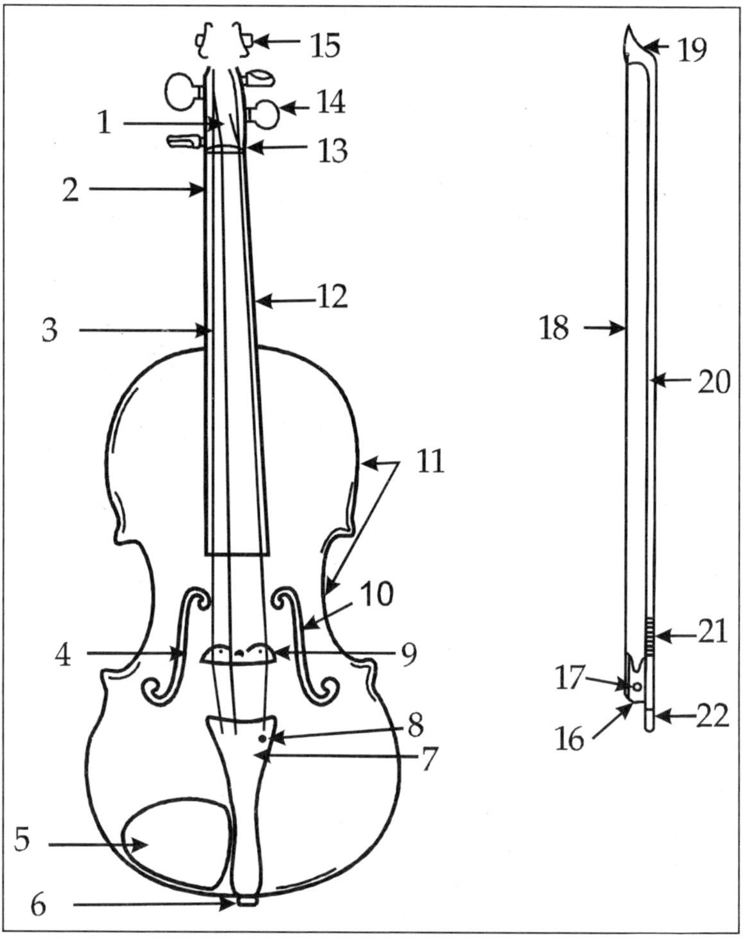


*fig.* 6.7: Violin (Diagrammatic)

on a bridge and finally attached to adjusting knobs situated at the other end of the finger board. It does not contain *pardās*. The instrument is played with the help of a bow. Different *svars* are produced by pressing the strings on the finger board by the fingers of the left hand while the right hand controls the movement of the bow. This instrument is used in solo performance and also as an accompaniment to vocal performance. This instrument is more popular in southern part of India.

### 6.13 Sāraṅgī

This is a string instrument which is played by using a bow. It is made from a rectangular piece of wood. The lower end of the wood is hollow and is covered with the skin of some animal. The strings are of metal and some of these are made from intestines of certain animals. Such strings on bowing produce *svars* of *mandra̱-saptak*. The strings are tied at the base of the instrument and then attached to the adjusting knobs situated at the upper part of the *sāraṅgī*. The strings rest on a bridge placed at the lower part of the instrument. It has no *pardās*. The bow is used by the right hand while the fingers of the left hand slide over the strings to produce different *svars*. Although *sāraṅgī* can be played as a solo instrument, it is the best accompaniment with singing. Its sound is quite close to human voice which makes it the most suitable accompanying instrument for vocal music (see *fig*. 6.8). Some of the well-known *sāraṅgī* players are Gopal Mishra, Ram Narayan, Sabari Khan and Bundu Khan.

Different components of a *sāraṅgī* are as under:

1. Pegs for tuning gut strings (main strings) which differ in thickness.
2. Pegs for tuning *tarabs*. There are many *tarabs* made of

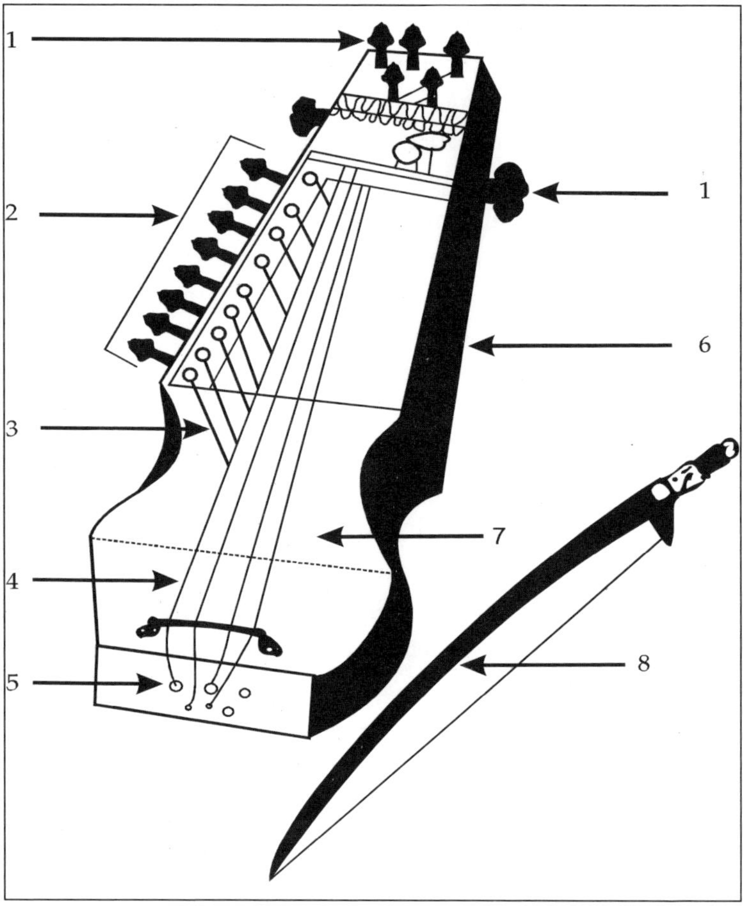


*fig.* 6.8: *Sāraṅgī* (Diagrammatic)

thin strings; these are placed beneath the main strings.

3. *Tarab*s (partly shown in the figure).
4. Main gut strings.
5. Peg for fastening strings.
6. Hollow wooden body of the instrument (about 2 ft long and 6 inches wide).

7. Parchment covering the hollow structure.
8. Bow.

### 6.14 Isrāj

This is a string instrument played with a bow. It is also known as *dilrubā.* This instrument can be regarded as a combination of *sitār* and *sāraṅgī.* Its shape is rectangular like *sāraṅgī* but is

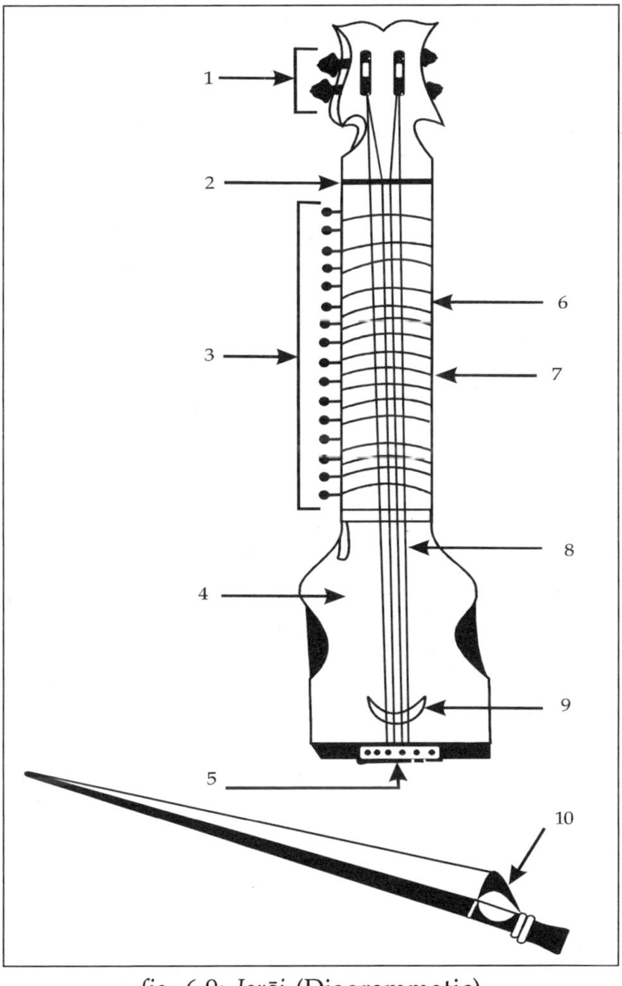


*fig.* 6.9: *Isrāj* (Diagrammatic)

comparatively longer. Its *daṇḍ* contains *pardā* (like *sitār* but unlike *sāraṅgī*) and is played with a bow (like *sāraṅgī* but unlike *sitār*). It has 16 *pardā*s and 4 strings. The bow is played with the right hand while the index and middle fingers of the left hand are moved on the strings to produce the desired *svar*s (see *fig*. 6.9).

Different components of an *isrāj* are as under:

1. Pegs for tuning the main strings.
2. Plate on which main strings rest.
3. Pegs for tuning sympathetic strings or *tarab*s (not shown in the figure) which lie beneath the main strings.
4. *Tūmbā*, whose upper part is covered with thin leather.
5. Nails for fastening strings.
6. *Daṇḍ*.
7. *Pardā*s or frets.
8. Main strings.
9. Bridge on which strings are stretched.
10. Bow called *gaẓ*.

### 6.15 Pakhāvaj

This is an *avanaddh vādya̱*. Lord Śiva̱'s *ḍamrū* is supposed to be the oldest *avanaddh vādya̱* from which other *avanaddh-vādya̱s* have originated.

*Pakhāvaj* is an old *avanaddh-vādya̱* which is also known as *mr̥daṅg, mārdal, muraj* or *khol*. *Mr̥daṅg* has been more popular in south India where it is known as *mr̥daṅgam*. The north Indian version of *mr̥daṅgam* is called *pakhāvaj*. It is used as an accompaniment to *dhrupad* singing. Since *dhrupad* singing has become rare, the use of *pakhāvaj* is also rare. Unlike *tablā*, *pakhāvaj* is a one-piece instrument. It consists of a hollow wooden structure cylindrical in shape. The diameter of one open end is bigger than that of the other open end. The two ends are covered with the skin of some animal. These covers or *pūḍīs* are tied to each other by leather straps. These straps are used to adjust the tension of the *pūḍīs* covering the two

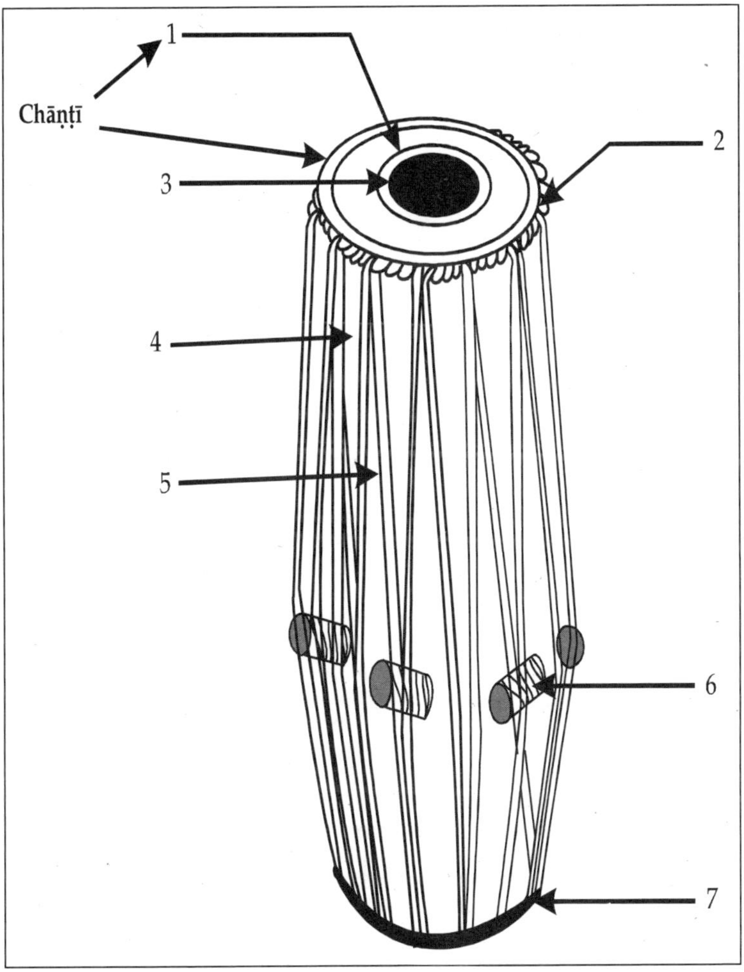


*fig.* 6.10: *Pakhāvaj* (Diagrammatic)

ends. Different *bols* come out of *pakhāvaj* when one or the other or both the *pūḍīs* are struck with hands. A *tāl* is created by the combination of the *bols*. Very complicated *tāls* such as Brahma̱, Rūdra, Viṣṇu, Lakṣmī *tāl*, etc. are played on *pakhāvaj* (see *fig*. 6.10). Some of the eminent *pakhāvaj* players are Nana Panse, Pagal Das and Ayodhya Prasad.

Different components of a *pakhāvaj* are as under:

1. *Chāṇṭī*.
2. *Gajarā*.
3. *Siāhī* (black paste which is allowed to dry).
4. Hollowed wooden cylinder: the two openings of the structure (which differ in size) are covered with skin of some animal; these are the two faces of the instrument.
5. Leather braces which run along the length of the cylindrical structure and hold the two faces.
6. Solid cylindrical wooden pieces called *gaṭṭā*. By moving these, the tension of leather braces can be adjusted to tune the instrument.
7. The other face of the *pakhāvaj*.

### 6.16 Tablā

This is the most important *avanaddh-vādya̱*. There are different views about the origin of *tablā*. According to one view, in the thirteenth century Amīr Khusro made *tablā* by cutting the *pakhāvaj* into two pieces. The word *tablā* is derived from a Farsi (Persian) word *tabl* meaning drum. Another view is that Sidhār Khān of Delhi designed the *tablā*.

During the last about 400 years, *khayāl* singing is increasingly becoming popular and now it has almost totally replaced the *dhrupad* style of singing. In *khayāl-gāyakī*, *tablā* is

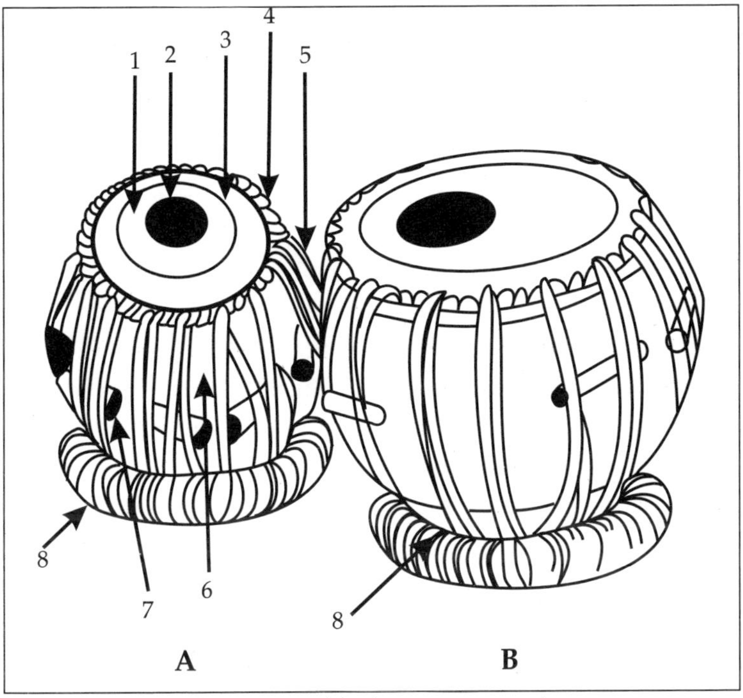


*fig.* 6.11: *Tablā* (Diagrammatic)

used as an accompanying instrument. This is the reason why the *tablā* has become an essential part of singing in Hindustani classical and also light music.

## *6.16.1 The Structure of Tablā*

The full form of *tablā* is *tablā-joḍī* because it contains two pieces. One is made of a hollow wooden structure called *tablā* (*fig.* 6.11A). Its open part is covered with the skin of an animal is called *puḍī*. The central part of the *pūḍī* is covered with a black paste called *siāhī*. The circumference of the *pūḍī* is covered with a leather strip called *chāṇṭī*. *Pūḍī* is fixed on the wooden structure through *gajarā* which is circular in shape and is made of small strips of leather. The *gajarā* and the lower part of the wooden structure are connected with leather strips called *baddhī*. The tension of *baddhī* can be adjusted by using wooden blocks called *gaṭṭā*. This part is played by the right hand hence it is called *dāyāṅ* or *tablā* (*fig*. 6.11 A).

The other part is wider than the *dāyāṅ* and is made of a metal or mud. Since this part is played with the left hand, it is called *bāyāṅ or daggā* (*fig*. 6.11 B). The upper open end of *daggā* is also covered with skin of some animal to which *siāhī* is applied. The *tablā* and *daggā* produce different kinds of sound. By striking only *tablā* or only *daggā* or both by the fingers different *bol*s such as Dhā, Nā, Dhin, Tin, Tū, etc. are produced. The combination of these *bol*s according to different schemes gives rise to what are known as *tāl*s (see *fig*. 6.11).

*Tablā* also has a number of *gharānā*s which have been named after the place where a particular style of *tablā* playing has been developed such as Delhi, Banāras, Lucknow, Punjābī, Ajrādā, Farukhābād Gharānā, etc. *Tablā* is also used in solo performance. Some of the eminent *tablā* players are Shamta Prasad, Kanthe Maharaj, Ram Sahaya, Ahmad Jan Thirakwa, Kishan Maharaj, Allarakha, Chatur Lal, Anokhe Lal, Manik Rao Popatkar, Nikhil Ghosh, Shafakat Hussain and Zakir Hussain.

Different components of a *tablā* are as under:

1. *Lav*,
2. *Siāhī*,
3. *Chāṇṭī*,
4. *Gajarā*,
5. *Baddhī* (leather strip),
6. Hollowed wooden structure,
7. Solid cylindrical wooden pieces called *gaṭṭā*,
8. *Gudṛī*, the base of the instrument.

Apart from *pakhāvaj* and *tablā*, several other kinds of *avanaddh vādyas* are also used in folk and film music.

### 6.17 Vaṅśī

*Vaṅśī* is a very old musical instrument which belongs to *suṣir-vādya* category. It is also known as *muralī* or *baṅsurī*. In English it is called flute. In old times *vaṅśī* was made from a small piece of bamboo of about 1"–2" diameter and having length from 1 to 2 ft. But now flutes made of brass and plastic are

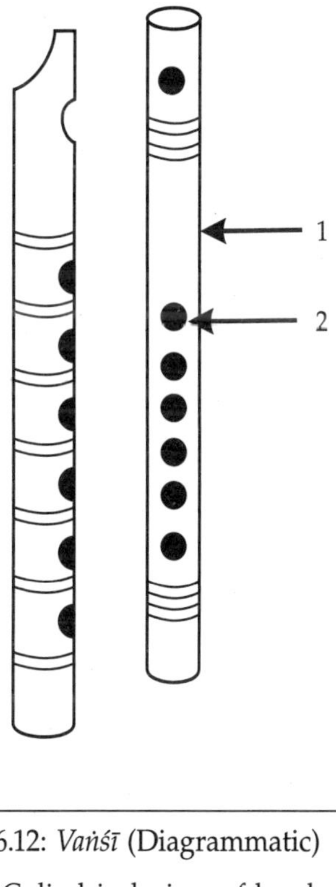


*fig.* 6.12: *Vaṅśī* (Diagrammatic)

1. Cylindrical piece of bamboo
2. Holes

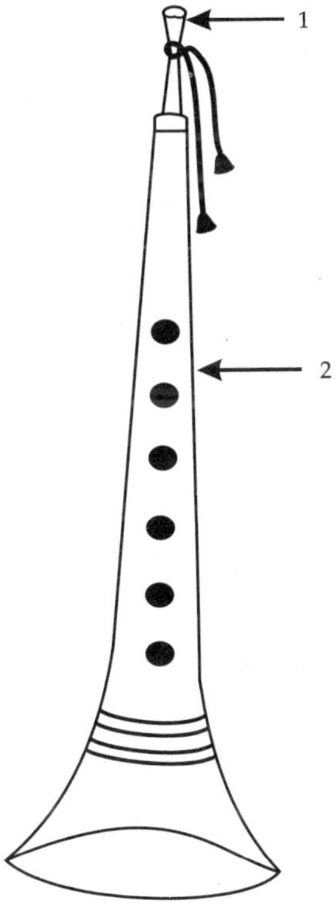


*fig.* 6.13: *Śahnāī* (Diagrammatic)

1. Reed
2. Hollow wooden structure

also available. A flute has six holes at different positions of the hollow tube. Air from the mouth is blown into the flute which then produces the sound. By closing the different holes of the flute by fingers, different *svar*s can be obtained. In some flutes, air is blown by keeping it straight while in some flutes, it is kept horizontal (see *fig*. 6.12). Flute is used in solo performance and also as accompanying instrument to singing. Some of the eminent flutists are Panna Lal Ghosh, Devendra Modheshwar, and Hari Prasad Chaurasia.

### 6.18 Śahnāī

This is also a *suṣir-vādya̱*. Its structure is like a flute. It consists of a hollow piece of wood having holes at different places. At the upper end of *śahnāī,* two chips of some material are placed which act as a reed. When air is blown into the instrument, sound is produced as a result of vibration of these chips. The sound of *śahnāī* resembles to some extent to that of clarinet. By closing the different holes of *śahnāī* with fingers, different *svar*s are obtained (see *fig*. 6.13). Previously this instrument was used during festivals or in palaces and temples but now it is played during music concerts. Bismillah Khan is the foremost *śahnāī* player who has made great contribution in promoting this instrument.

### 6.19 Ghan-Vādya̱

In these instruments pieces of metals or wood are struck with sticks to produce different *svar*s. Examples of some *ghan-vādya̱*s are given below:

(i) ***Bell***: In temples these are used to produce metallic sound during *pūjā*.[10] The quality of sound depends upon the size and shape of the bell.

10. Worship.

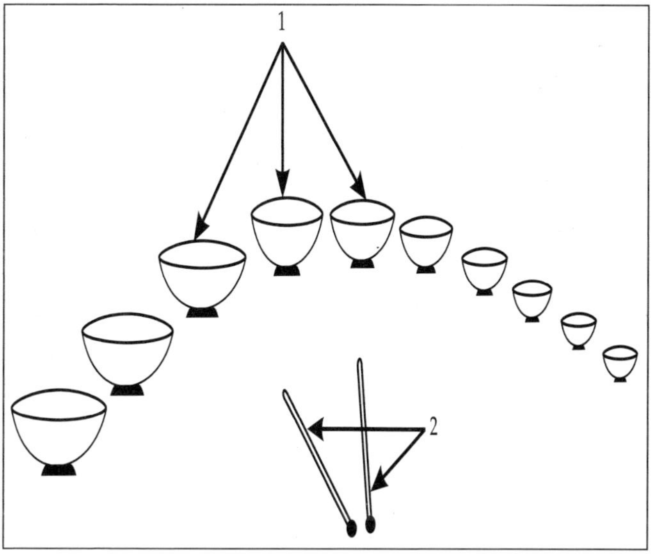


*fig.* 6.14: *Jal-Taraṅg* (Diagrammatic)

(ii) ***Khaṛtāls*** are used during *kīrtan*. These are made of wooden pieces containing metallic foils. On shaking *khaṛtāls*, in a particular *laya̱*, a rhythmic, pleasant sound is produced.

(iii) ***Ghaṇṭā-taraṅg***: This consists of a rectangular wooden framework which holds a number of circular metallic plates made of bronze or brass. These plates are of different sizes. When these are struck by wooden or metallic sticks different *svar*s are obtained to play a *rāg* or a tune *(dhun)*.

(iv) ***Kāṣṭha̱-taraṅg***: In this instrument wooden pieces of different sizes are placed vertically on two pieces of wooden sticks parallel to each other. It is played by striking these pieces by wooden sticks.

(v) ***Nal-taraṅg***: This consists of several hollow steel tubes of different lengths which, on striking, produce various *svars*.

(vi) ***Jal-taraṅg***: This is a very melodious instrument but now is very rarely used. In this instrument there are about 12 to 15 bowls made of China clay. Different sizes of bowls are filled with different quantities of water. By adjusting the amount of water different *svar*s can be produced on striking the bowls. Thus a *rāg* can be played on this instrument (see *fig*. 6.14).

Different components of *jal-taraṅg* are as under:

1. China clay pots of various sizes containing suitable amounts of water.
2. Wooden strikers.

# 7

# Description of Certain Famous Rāgs of Hindustani Music

In Hindustani classical music 10 *thāṭ*s have been selected for the classification of various *rāg*s. Theoretically several thousand *rāg*s can be formed by the permutation and combination of the different musical notes or *svar*s of these *thāṭ*s. However, in actual practice, a much smaller number of *rāg*s, say, around 150 are normally performed in musical concerts. In this chapter the characteristics of some famous *rāg*s have been described.

The foremost important thing to know is the *thāṭ* in which the *rāg* under consideration has been placed. After this, comes *jāti, āroh, avaroh, vādī* and *saṁvādī svar*s of the *rāg*.

There are many *rāg*s which use more or less similar *svar*s. In such cases, it is extremely necessary to sing frequently those particular groups of *svar*s which characterise the *rāg* being sung. Such groups of *svar*s are referred to as *pakaḍ* of the *rāg*. The term *pakaḍ* may thus be defined as the group of *svar*s sung in a particular sequence so as to make it clear to the listeners the *rāg* which is being presented. In fact, while rendering any *rāg*, *pakaḍ* is used for the identification of the *rāg*.

Another important term that has to be understood is *svar-vistār*. It means developing various combinations of the *svar*s of the *rāg* so as to create a melodious atmosphere, at the same time keeping in mind the rules prescribed for singing the given *rāg*. A *rāg* consists of 5, 6 or 7 *svar*s only, but a proficient singer can sing the *rāg* for one to two hours. This is possible only if the performer has good musical sense and rich imagination which is the essence of *khayāl* singing (*khayāl* means imagination).

*Svar-vistār*s given in this chapter are those described by Pandit V.N. Bhatkhande.

*Svar-vistār* involves the use of *svar*s of the *rāg* in an ascending or descending manner or by mixing the two processes and extending this exercise to all the three *saptak*s namely *mandra̲*, *madhya̲* and *tār-saptak*. If the note-combinations mentioned in the *svar-vistār* of a *rāg* are uttered correctly even by a beginner, the *svarūp* (framework and mood) of the *rāg* will at once emerge and one would be able to recognise the *rāg*.

For every *rāg*, a particular time of the day or night is allotted in musical texts — this has also been given in the following description of the *rāg*s (see section 2.14).

### 7.1 Rāg Ābhogī

| | | |
|---|---|---|
| (i) | Base *thāṭ* | *Kāfī* |
| (ii) | *Jāti* | *Ouḍav – Ouḍav* |
| (iii) | *Āroh* | S R G̲ M D Ṡ |
| (iv) | *Avaroh* | Ṡ D M G̲ R S |
| (v) | *Vādī* | S |
| (vi) | *Saṁvādī* | M |
| (vii) | *Pakaḍ* | M G̲ Ṛ Ṣ, Ḍ Ḍ Ṣ, S, M, M M D G̲, M G̲ M D, Ṡ, Ṡ, Ṡ D Ṡ, D, M D, G̲ |
| (viii) | Singing time | Morning |

### *Svar-vistār*

(a) <u>G</u> R S, Ḍ S, R <u>G</u> M, D M <u>G</u>, R S, <u>G</u> M D Ṡ, D Ṡ D M, <u>G</u> R S, Ḍ Ḍ S

(b) D, M D, S R <u>G</u> M D, Ṡ D, Ṙ D, <u>Ġ</u> Ṙ Ṡ D Ṡ, D, Ṁ <u>Ġ</u> Ṙ Ṡ D Ṡ, D, M D Ṡ D Ṡ, D <u>G</u>, M <u>G</u> R S, Ḍ Ḍ S

(c) S <u>G</u> M, <u>G</u> M D M D Ṡ, D Ṡ Ṁ <u>Ġ</u> Ṙ Ṡ, M D Ṡ D M <u>G</u>, Ṡ D M <u>G</u>, M D M <u>G</u>, M <u>G</u> R S

### *Remarks*

This is a Karnatic *rāg* from south India, which has been incorporated in the north Indian classical music. *Ṣaḍj<u>a</u>* is the *nyās svar* in this *rāg* (*nyās svar* is that at which a singer can stay for a while, during the presentation of a *rāg;* it is also known as rest note).

## 7.2 Rāg Ahīr-Bhairav

| | | |
|---|---|---|
| (i) | Base *thāṭ* | *Bhairav* |
| (ii) | *Jāti* | *Sampūrṇ<u>a</u> – Sampūrṇ<u>a</u>* |
| (iii) | *Āroh* | S <u>R</u> G M P D <u>N</u> Ṡ |
| (iv) | *Avaroh* | Ṡ <u>N</u> D P M G <u>R</u> S |
| (v) | *Vādī* | M |
| (vi) | *Saṁvādī* | S |
| (vii) | *Pakaḍ* | G, M, <u>R</u>, S, <u>R</u> G, M, P, D <u>N</u> D, P, M P, M G, M <u>R</u>, S. |
| (viii) | Singing time | Morning 4 – 7 a.m. |

### *Svar-vistār*

(a) G G, <u>R</u> S, S S <u>R</u> S, S <u>R</u> S, <u>Ṇ</u> S G <u>R</u>, G G M, G M <u>R</u> P, G M <u>R</u> S.

(b) M M <u>R</u> M, P P M P, P M P D, <u>N</u> D P D, M P G M, <u>R</u> <u>R</u> G M, P G <u>R</u> S.

(c) <u>R</u> <u>R</u> S S, G <u>R</u> G M, M M P G, M <u>R</u> <u>R</u>, S, S <u>R</u> S M, G <u>R</u> S P, G M P G, M G <u>R</u> S.

*Remarks*

1. This is one of the varieties of the *Bhairav rāg.*
2. Although this *rāg* is not as old as *Bhairav,* it has become more popular than *Bhairav* itself.
3. Some people regard this *rāg* to be a mixture of the *Bhairav* and *Kāfī thāṭs* while some treat it as a combination of *Bhairav* and *Khamāj thāṭ*. Since the *Bhairav* part is more dominating, *rāg Ahīr-Bhairav* is kept under *Bhairav thāṭ.*
4. *Pañcham* is weak in the *āroh* and certain singers do not use it in the *avaroh.*
5. This is a morning *sandhi-prakāś rāg*, which has R̲ and M.
6. *Viśrānti* (staying) at the M sounds very pleasant while singing this *rāg*. Thus M will be the *nyās svar* or rest note.

**7.3 Rāg Bāgeśwarī**

| (i) | Base *thāṭ* | *Kāfī* |
|---|---|---|
| (ii) | *Jāti* | *Ouḍav — Ṣāḍav* |
| (iii) | *Āroh* | S, M G̲, M D, N̲ Ṡ |
| (iv) | *Avaroh* | Ṡ, N̲ D, M G̲, M G̲ R S |
| (v) | *Vādī* | M |
| (vi) | *Saṁvādī* | S |
| (vii) | *Pakaḍ* | S, Ṇ̲ Ḍ, S, M D N̲ D, M, G̲ R, S |
| (viii) | Singing time | Midnight |

*Svar-vistār*

(a) S, R S, Ṇ̲ Ḍ, S, M G̲, M D, M G̲, M G̲ R S.

(b) S, Ṇ̲ S, M G̲, D M G̲, N̲ D, M G̲, Ṡ, N̲ D, M G̲, M D N̲ D, M G̲, M G̲ R S.

(c) $\underset{\cdot}{\underline{N}}$ S $\underline{G}$, M $\underline{G}$, D M $\underline{G}$, $\underline{N}$ $\underline{N}$ D M $\underline{G}$, $\dot{S}$ $\underline{N}$ D M $\underline{G}$, $\dot{R}$ $\dot{S}$, $\underline{N}$ D M D $\underline{N}$ D M $\underline{G}$, D M $\underline{G}$, M $\underline{G}$, M $\underline{G}$ R S.

*Remarks*

1. It is a very old and melodious *rāg* which uses $\underline{G}$, $\underline{N}$. Rest of the *svars* are *śuddh*.

2. There are different opinions regarding the use of P:
   (a) It is totally forbidden — that would make this *rāg* *Ṣāḍav.*
   (b) P is forbidden in the *āroh* — that would make the *rāg Ṣāḍav — Sampūrṇa̲.*
   (c) P is used in *āroh* as well as in *avaroh* — that would make the *rāg Sampūrṇa̲.*

Generally R and P are very rarely used in the *āroh* and can be treated as forbidden. P is generally forbidden in the *avaroh* so that the *rāg* is known as *Ouḍav-Ṣāḍav.* However, some singers use P in the *avaroh,* in that case the *rāg* will become *Ouḍav-Sampūrṇa̲.* But normally P is not used in the *avaroh,* hence the *rāg* should be termed *Ouḍav Ṣāḍav.*

3. M D $\underline{N}$ note-combination is a very important part of this *rāg.*

### 7.4 Rāg Bhairavī

| | | |
|---|---|---|
| (i) | Base *thāṭ* | *Bhairavī* |
| (ii) | *Jāti* | *Sampūrṇa̲ — Sampūrṇa̲* |
| (iii) | *Āroh* | S $\underline{R}$ $\underline{G}$ M P $\underline{D}$ $\underline{N}$ $\dot{S}$ |
| (iv) | *Avaroh* | $\dot{S}$ $\underline{N}$ $\underline{D}$ P M $\underline{G}$ $\underline{R}$ S |
| (v) | *Vādī* | M |
| (vi) | *Saṁvādī* | S |
| (vii) | *Pakaḍ* | M, $\underline{G}$, S $\underline{R}$ S, $\underset{\cdot}{\underline{D}}$ $\underset{\cdot}{\underline{N}}$ S |
| (viii) | Singing time | Morning (can be sung at any time.) |

## *Svar-vistār*

(a) G̲, S R̲ S, Ḍ̲, Ṇ̲, S, G̲, M G̲ R̲ S.

(b) S, Ṇ̲ S, Ḍ̲, Ṇ̲ S, G̲, M G̲, P M G̲, R̲ S, M G̲ R̲, S.

(c) Ṇ̲ S G̲, R̲ G̲, M G̲, P M G̲, P D̲ M P G̲, N̲ N̲ D̲ D̲ P D̲ M P G̲, Ṡ, N̲, D̲, P, D̲ M P G̲, R̲ S, R̲ G̲, M G̲ R̲ S.

## *Remarks*

1. This is a very popular *rāg* which is the *āśrya̲* *rāg* of *thāṭ Bhairavī*.
2. Although it is a morning *rāg*, practically it is sung at any time of the day or night. Generally, singers conclude their programme by singing a *bandiś* in *Bhairavī*.
3. There is a difference of opinion regarding the *vādī* and *saṁvādī svar* of this *rāg*. Some musicians use M as *vādī* and S as *saṁvādī* while some regard D as *vādī* and G as *saṁvādī*.
4. Some singers use R. In that case this *rāg* is known as *Sindhu Bhairavī*.
5. While singing *Bhairavī* expert singers use all the twelve *svar*s to create melody and to entertain the audience.
6. This *rāg* is very rarely sung in the form of a *khayāl*. Mostly *ṭhumrīs*, *ṭappās*, *bhajans*, *ghazal*s and *gīt* are sung in the *rāg Bhairavī*.

### 7.5 Rāg Bhīmpalāsī

| (i) | Base *thāṭ* | *Kāfī* |
|---|---|---|
| (ii) | *Jāti* | *Ouḍav — Sampūrṇa̲* |
| (iii) | *Āroh* | Ṇ̲ S G̲ M, P, N̲ Ṡ |
| (iv) | *Avaroh* | Ṡ N̲ D P M G̲ R S |
| (v) | *Vādī* | M |
| (vi) | *Saṁvādī* | S |
| (vii) | *Pakaḍ* | N̲ S M, M G̲, P M, G̲, M G̲ R S |
| (viii) | Singing time | 1 p.m. to 4 p.m. |

## *Svar-vistār*

(a) S, N̲̣ S, M, M, P G̲, M, P, N̲ D P, M P, G̲, M, P G̲, M G̲ R S, N̲̣ S, G̲ R S.

(b) N̲̣, S, P̣ N̲̣, S, M G̲ R S, N̲̣ S G̲ M P G̲, M G̲ R S, N̲ D P, M P, G̲ M, P G̲, M G̲ R S.

(c) S, N̲̣ N̲̣ S, M, G̲, M, P, M, D P, M P G̲, M, Ṡ, P D P, M P, G̲, M, Ṙ Ṡ, N̲ D P, Ṡ N̲ D P, N̲ D P, M P, G̲, M, P G̲, M G̲ R S.

## *Remarks*

1. *Rāg Bāgeśwarī* is the *chhāyā-lag rāg* (see section 2.13.2) of *Bhīmpalāsī.* The two *rāgs* can be differentiated by using the note-combinations shown below.

   *Bhīmpalāsī* : S, N̲̣ S M, M P G̲ M, G̲ R S.

   *Bāgeśwarī* : Ṃ Ḍ N̲̣ S M, G̲ M D, M P D G̲, M G̲ R S.

   There is another *rāg,* namely *Dhanāśrī* which has the same *āroh* and *avaroh* as in *Bhīmpalāsī,* but in *Dhanāśrī,* the *vādī* is P whereas in *Bhīmpalāsī,* M is the *vādī svar.* If the *rāg Bhīmpalāsī* is sung using N instead of N̲, the resultant *rāg* is *Paṭdīp.*

### 7.6 Rāg Bhūpālī

| | | |
|---|---|---|
| (i) | Base *thāṭ* | *Kalyāṇ* |
| (ii) | *Jāti* | *Ouḍav — Ouḍav* |
| (iii) | *Āroh* | S R G P, D, Ṡ |
| (iv) | *Avaroh* | Ṡ D P, G, R, S |
| (v) | *Vādī* | G |
| (vi) | *Saṁvādī* | D |
| (vii) | *Pakaḍ* | G, R, S, Ḍ, S R G, P G, D P G, R, S |
| (viii) | Singing time | First part of the night (7–10 p.m.) |

*Svar-vistār*

(a) G, R, S, S Ḍ, S R G, R G, P G, D P G, R G, G, R, S, S Ḍ, S R G.

(b) S, G, R G, S R G, P̣ Ḍ S R G, G P G, G P D P G, P G, R G, R, S, Ḍ, S R G.

(c) S R G, R G, Ḍ Ḍ S R G, P G, D P G, G P D Ṡ D P G, G P D Ṡ, Ṙ Ṡ D P G, Ṡ, D P G, D P G, R G, P, R, S, Ḍ, R, S.

*Remarks*

If D is too much emphasised the shadow of the *rāg Deśkār* would creep in. This is due to the fact that the *vādī* and *saṁvādī* in *Bhūpālī* are G and D respectively while in *Deśkār* the order is reversed. The other features of the two *rāg*s are similar.

### 7.7 Rāg Bihāg

| (i) | Base *thāṭ* | *Bilāwal* |
|---|---|---|
| (ii) | *Jāti* | *Ouḍav – Sampūrṇa* |
| (iii) | *Āroh* | S G M P N Ṡ |
| (iv) | *Avaroh* | Ṡ N D P M G R S |
| (v) | *Vādī* | G |
| (vi) | *Saṁvādī* | N |
| (vii) | *Pakaḍ* | Ṇ S, G M P, G M G, R S |
| (viii) | Singing time | Late night, say, 10 p.m. to 1 a.m. |

*Svar-vistār*

(a) G, R S, Ṇ, S, G, M G, P, G M G, R S, S, R S.

(b) Ṇ P̣, Ṇ, S, G S, G M G S, Ṇ S G M P G M G, S, Ṇ S G M P, N P, M̍P, G M G, S G, M P G M G, R S, Ṇ R S.

(c) Ṇ S G, S, G, M G, P, G M G, N, P, G M G, Ṡ, N P, G M G, G M P G M G, R S, Ṇ, R S.

### *Remarks*

1. *In Bihāg,* M̍ is used as a *vivādī svar.* This *rāg* is sung in the night, and the night *rāgs* generally use M̍. This is the reason why the use of M̍ in *Bihāg* enhances the melody of the *rāg*. These days most of the singers freely use M̍ while singing the *rāg Bihāg.*

2. Some singers do not use R and D at all, while some use these *svars* rarely in the *avaroh.* If emphasis on R and D is more in the *avaroh,* there would be a shadow of the *rāg Bilāwal* on the *rāg Bihāg.*

## 7.8 Rāg Brandāvanī Sāraṅg

| (i) | Base *thāṭ* | *Kāfī* |
|---|---|---|
| (ii) | *Jāti* | *Ouḍav – Ouḍav* |
| (iii) | *Āroh* | Ṇ S, R, M P, N Ṡ |
| (iv) | *Avaroh* | Ṡ N̲ P M R S |
| (v) | *Vādī* | R |
| (vi) | *Saṁvādī* | P |
| (vii) | *Pakaḍ* | Ṇ S R, M R, P M R, S. |
| (viii) | Singing time | Noon |

### *Svar-vistār*

(a) S, Ṇ S, R, M R, P R, M P, N̲ P M R, R M P M R, R, S.

(b) S, Ṇ S, R M R S, P M R S, R M P, M P, N̲ P, M P N̲ P M R, P M R, M R, S.

### *Remarks*

1. In this *rāg* G and D are not used.

2. N is used in the *āroh* and N̲ is used in the *avaroh.*

3. Singers normally stay on *svars* S, R and P; these are the rest notes.

4. According to some musicians this *rāg* should be kept under *Khamāj thāṭ.*

## 7.9 Rāg Deśa̲

| (i) | Base *thāṭ* | *Khamāj* |
|---|---|---|
| (ii) | *Jāti* | *Ouḍav – Sampūrṇa̲* |
| (iii) | *Āroh* | S R M P N Ṡ |
| (iv) | *Avaroh* | Ṡ N̲ D P, M G, R G, S |
| (v) | *Vādī* | R |
| (vi) | *Saṁvādī* | P |
| (vii) | *Pakaḍ* | R, M P, N̲ D P, P D P M, G R G S |
| (viii) | Singing time | Midnight |

*Svar-vistār*

(a) R R, M P, N̲ D P, P D P M G R G S, R R M P, N̲ D P.

(b) S, Ṇ S, R R, R G R M G R, P M G R, N̲ N̲ D P, M P D M G R, P M G R, G S, R R M P, N̲ D P.

(c) S, Ṇ S, R R, M G R, P M G R, M P D M G R, P M G R M G R, G S, R R M P, N̲ D P.

*Remarks*

1. Both the varieties of *niṣād*, namely *komal* (N̲) and *tīvra̲* (N) are used in this *rāg*. Generally N is used in the *āroh* and N̲ in the *avaroh*, like M P N Ṡ, N̲ D P, D M G R.
2. This *rāg* is extensively used for singing *ṭhumrī* when G and D are also sometimes touched in *āroh* to increase the sweetness of the *rāg*.
3. In the *avaroh* of this *rāg*, R is used in a *vakra̲* manner, e.g. G R G S (see section 3.9, xxxi).
4. Some singers regard P as *vādī* and R as *saṁvādī*.
5. *Rāg Deśa̲* and *rāg Soraṭh* are of the same nature. In *Deśa̲* G is distinctly used but in *Soraṭh* G is used in a subtle manner.

### 7.10 Rāg Gūjarī Toḍī

| (i) | Base *thāṭ* | *Toḍī* |
|---|---|---|
| (ii) | *Jāti* | *Ṣāḍav – Ṣāḍav* |
| (iii) | *Āroh* | S R̲ G̲ M̍ D̲ N Ṡ |
| (iv) | *Avaroh* | Ṡ N D̲ M̍ G̲ R̲ S |
| (v) | *Vādī* | D̲ |
| (vi) | *Saṁvādī* | R̲ OR G̲ |
| (vii) | *Pakaḍ* | G̲, R̲ S, Ṇ S, R̲ G̲, R̲ G̲, M̍G̲ D̲ M̍G̲, R̲ G̲, R̲ S, Ṇ R̲, S. |
| (viii) | Singing time | Noon, say, 10 a.m. to 1 p.m. |

*Svar-vistār*

(a) Ṇ S G̲ R̲ S, Ṇ, R̲ Ṇ D̲̣, Ṃ̍ D̲̣ Ṇ S, D̲̣ Ṇ S, R̲, G̲, M̍ G̲, D̲M̍ G̲ N D̲ M̍ G̲, R̲ G̲, R̲ S.

(b) M̍ G̲ M̍ D̲, Ṙ̲, Ṡ N, Ṡ Ṙ̲ Ġ̲ Ṙ̲ Ṡ, N N Ṡ Ṙ̲ N D̲, Ġ̲, Ṙ̲, Ṡ, N, Ṡ Ṙ̲, N D̲, M̍ D̲, M̍ M̍ G̲ G̲, M̍ D̲, Ṙ̲, N D̲, M̍ D̲, M̍ G̲, R̲ G̲, R̲ S.

*Remarks*

1. Some singers regard R̲ as *saṁvādī svar* while some books recommend G̲ as the *saṁvādī svar*.
2. This *rāg* has been derived from *rāg Toḍī* by deleting the note P from the parent *rāg*, i.e. *Toḍī*.

### 7.11 Rāg Kedār

| (i) | Base *thāṭ* | *Kalyāṇ* |
|---|---|---|
| (ii) | *Jāti* | *Ouḍav – Sampūrṇa* |
| (iii) | *Āroh* | S M, M P, D P, N D, Ṡ |
| (iv) | *Avaroh* | Ṡ, N D, P, M̍ P D P, M, G M R S |
| (v) | *Vādī* | M |
| (vi) | *Saṁvādī* | S |
| (vii) | *Pakaḍ* | S, M, M P, D P M, P M, R S |
| (viii) | Singing time | First part of night 7 – 10 p.m. |

### *Svar-vistār*

(a) S M, M P, P D, P, M, M P D P M, P M, M, R, S, S R, S.

(b) P̣ P̣ S, Ḍ S, R S, Ṃ Ṃ P̣ P̣ S, Ṃ P̣ S, P̣ S, R S, M M R S, S M P D P M R S, Ṡ, D P, M̍ P D P M M R S, S R S.

(c) S M G P, P, M̍ P, D D P P, N N D D P P, M̍ P D N̲ D P M̍ P D P M, M̍ Ṁ Ṙ Ṡ, N D P M̍ P Ṡ, N D P M̍ P, D P M, S M, P, D P M, P M, R S.

### *Remarks*

1. In this *rāg*, both the varieties of M are used in the *avaroh*, M̍ is used along with P.
2. In the *āroh* one goes straight from S to M.
3. G is weak and *vakra̲* in *avaroh*, hence some people regard it to be *Ouḍav-Ṣāḍav rāg*.
4. Some singers scarcely use N̲ in *avaroh*, as *vivādī*.

## 7.12 Rāg Lalit

| | | |
|---|---|---|
| (i) | Base *thāṭ* | *Mārwā* |
| (ii) | *Jāti* | *Ṣāḍav – Ṣāḍav* |
| (iii) | *Āroh* | Ṇ R̲ G M, M̍ M G, M̍ D, Ṡ |
| (iv) | *Avaroh* | Ṙ̲ N D, M̍ D M̍ M G, R̲, S |
| (v) | *Vādī* | M |
| (vi) | *Saṁvādī* | S |
| (vii) | *Pakaḍ* | Ṇ R̲ G M, D M̍ D M̍ M, G |
| (viii) | Singing time | 1 a.m. – 4 a.m. |

### *Svar-vistār*

(a) G, R̲ S, Ṇ R̲ G M, G, M, M̍, M, M̍ G, R̲ G, M̍ G, G, R̲ S, Ṇ R̲ G, M.

(b) Ṇ S, R̲ S, G, M, S, G, M, G M, M̍ G, G, M̍ D, M̍ M, G M, D, M̍ M, G M, M̍, M, R̲ G, M̍ G, R̲ S, Ṇ R̲, G M.

*Remarks*

1. One of the most important features of this *rāg* is that both the varieties of the note M are sung one after another; this combination is extremely rare in the Indian *rāg* system.

2. Repeated use of the group of notes "D M̍ D M̍ M" makes the *rāg* very distinct.

3. Presently D̲ is used in this *rāg* in place of D; this makes the *rāg* more melodious. For this reason this *rāg* is sometimes kept under *Pūrvī thāṭ*.

### 7.13 Rāg Madhumād Sāraṅg

| | | |
|---|---|---|
| (i) | Base *thāṭ* | *Kāfī* |
| (ii) | *Jāti* | *Ouḍav – Ouḍav* |
| (iii) | *Āroh* | S R M P N̲ Ṡ |
| iv) | *Avaroh* | Ṡ N̲ P M R S |
| (v) | *Vādī* | R |
| (vi) | *Saṁvādī* | P |
| (vii) | *Pakaḍ* | R, M P, N̲, Ṡ, N̲ P M R, S |
| (viii) | Singing time | 10 a.m. – 1 p.m. |

*Svar-vistār*

(a) S, N̲̣ S, R, M R, P R, S, N̲̣ S, P̣ N̲̣, P̣ N̲̣ S, Ṃ P̣ N̲̣ S, R, N̲̣ S, R M P, M, P, R, P R, N̲̣ S.

(b) N̲̣, S, P̣ N̲̣ S, Ṃ P̣ N̲̣ S, S, R, P R, M P N̲ N̲ P M R Ṡ, N̲, P, M R, P R, S.

*Remarks*

1. It is also called *Madhyamād Sāraṅg* or *Madhyamādi Sāraṅg* — and is a variety of the *rāg Sāraṅg*.

2. According to certain books this *rāg* is supposed to be derived from *Khamāj thāṭ*.

3. The note-combination PR and N̲P is the highlight of this *rāg*.

4. Upon using both the *niṣāds*, *tīvra̲* N in *āroh* and *komal* N in *avaroh* and also if the note R is emphasised, another *rāg*, namely *Brandāvanī Sāraṅg* is created.

5. This *rāg* is quite similar to *rāg Megh* but the two *rāgs* can be differentiated by the way these are sung.

## 7.14 Rāg Madhuvantī

| | | |
|---|---|---|
| (i) | Base *thāṭ* | *Toḍī* |
| (ii) | *Jāti* | *Ouḍav – Sampūrṇa̲* |
| (iii) | *Āroh* | S G̲ M̍ P N Ṡ |
| (iv) | *Avaroh* | Ṡ N D P M̍ G̲ R S |
| (v) | *Vādī* | P |
| (vi) | *Saṁvādī* | R |
| (vii) | *Pakaḍ* | Ṇ S G̲ M̍ P, G̲ M̍ G̲ R S. |
| (viii) | Singing time | 4 p.m. to 7 p.m. |

*Svar-vistār*

(a) Ṇ S G̲ M̍ P, G̲ M̍ P N Ṡ, Ṡ N D P, M̍ P, G̲ M̍ G S R S, Ṇ Ḍ P̣, Ṃ̍ P̣ Ṇ S Ṇ S G̲ R S, G̲ M̍ P N P N Ṡ, P N Ṡ Ġ̲ Ṙ Ṡ, N D P, P D M̍ P G̲ M̍ P, G̲ S R S.

*Remarks*

1. The touch (*kaṇ*) of S on R and that of M̍ on G̲ enhances the sweetness of the *rāg*.

2. Some singers scarcely use N̲ also to produce an element of surprise. This experiment enhances the melody of the *rāg*.

3. The *chalan* (pattern) of this *rāg* is like that of *Multānī*. (*Multānī* uses R̲ and D̲ instead of R and D used in *Madhuvantī*).

## 7.15 Rāg Mālkauṅs

| (i) | Base *thāṭ* | *Bhairavī* |
|---|---|---|
| (ii) | *Jāti* | *Ouḍav – Ouḍav* |
| (iii) | *Āroh* | N̤ S, G M, D, N Ṡ |
| (iv) | *Avaroh* | Ṡ N D, M, G M G S |
| (v) | *Vādī* | M |
| (vi) | *Saṁvādī* | S |
| (vii) | *Pakaḍ* | M G, M D N D, M, G, S |
| viii) | Singing time | After midnight |

### *Svar-vistār*

(a) S, N̤ S, M, M G, M D, N D, M G, G M G, S.

(b) S, N̤ S, D̤ N̤ S, M M G, M D N D M G, M D N Ṡ N D M G, N D M G, D M G, G M G S.

(c) N̤ S, M, G M, D M, N D M, Ṡ N D M, Ġ Ṡ, N D M, N D, M, Ġ Ṁ Ġ Ṡ, N D, M, Ṡ N D M, G M G S.

### *Remarks*

1. It is a very popular and serious *rāg*.
2. If N is used in place of N then we get the *rāg Chandrakauṅs*.
3. It can be sung in all the three *saptaks*.
4. One can sing a *baḍā-khayāl, chhoṭā-khayāl, tarānā, dhrupad, dhamār* and *bhajans* in this *rāg*.
5. While singing this *rāg*, the first string of the accompanying*tānpūrā* is tuned to M as P is forbidden in this *rāg*.

### 7.16 Rāg Mārwā

| (i) | Base *thāṭ* | *Mārwā* |
|---|---|---|
| (ii) | *Jāti* | *Ṣāḍav – Ṣāḍav* |
| (iii) | *Āroh* | S R̲ G M̍ D, N D, Ṡ |
| (iv) | *Avaroh* | Ṡ N D, M̍ G R̲ S |
| (v) | *Vādī* | R̲ |
| (vi) | *Saṁvādī* | D |
| (vii) | *Pakaḍ* | D M̍ G R̲, G M̍ G, R̲ S |
| (viii) | Singing time | Evening 4 p.m. to 7 p.m. |

*Svar-vistār*

(a) G, R̲, S, Ṇ, R̲, S, Ṇ R̲ G, R̲ G, M̍ G, R̲, S

(b) S, Ṇ R̲ Ṇ Ḍ, Ṃ̍ Ḍ S, R̲, G R̲, M̍ G R̲, D M̍ G R̲, N D M̍, G R̲, G M̍ D, M̍ G R̲, G R̲, S, Ṇ, R̲, S.

(c) Ṡ D, D, N D, M̍ D, N D, M̍ G R̲, G M̍ D, N D, M̍ G, R̲, G, R̲ S.

*Remarks*

1. *Svars* R̲, G and D are important in this *rāg*. Peculiarity of this *rāg* is that unlike other *rāgs*, S is scarcely used especially in the *āroh*. The *r̥ṣabh* R̲ is used in a *vakra* manner such as R̲ M̍ G R̲, G R̲ M̍ G R̲, Ṇ R̲ S, etc.
2. While singing this *rāg* the first string of the accompanying *tānpūrā* is tuned to the N of the *mandra saptak* as P is forbidden in this *rāg*.
3. While singing this *rāg* the *svar-vistār* should be carefully followed otherwise the shadow of the *chhāyā-lag rāgs* namely *Pūriā* and *Sohnī* would be noticed (see section 2.13.2).
4. After singing the *rāg Mārwā*, one can smoothly move to the *rāgs* of the *Kalyāṇ thāṭ*, hence this is regarded as *Parmelpraveśak rāg* (see section 3.9, xlii).

## 7.17 Rāg Meghmalhār

| | | |
|---|---|---|
| (i) | Base *thāṭ* | *Kāfī* |
| (ii) | *Jāti* | *Ouḍav – Ouḍav* |
| (iii) | *Āroh* | S M R M P N̲ Ṡ |
| (iv) | *Avaroh* | Ṡ N̲ P M R M R, N̲̣ R S |
| (v) | *Vādī* | S |
| (vi) | *Saṁvādī* | P |
| (vii) | *Pakaḍ* | R M, R S, N̲̣ P̣, N̲̣ S, R, M R, P, R M, R, S. |
| (viii) | Singing time | During rainy season |

### *Svar-vistār*

(a) S N̲̣ S, N̲̣ S, R M R, S, N̲̣ S, P, M R, S, N̲ N̲ P, M P, M R, S.

(b) S, R S, N̲̣ N̲̣ P̣, Ṃ P̣ N̲̣ N̲̣ S, R, M R, N̲ P, Ṡ, N̲ P, M R, S.

### *Remarks*

1. Some singers use M as *saṁvādī svar.*
2. This *rāg* finds its origin in the ancient Indian music traditions.
3. The note-combination M R P is emphasised while rendering this *rāg.*
4. Singers stay on M to differentiate it from the *rāg Sāraṅg.*
5. Some singers use D also in this *rāg.*

## 7.18 Rāg Multānī

| | | |
|---|---|---|
| (i) | Base *thāṭ* | *Toḍī* |
| (ii) | *Jāti* | *Ouḍav – Sampūrṇa* |
| (iii) | *Āroh* | Ṇ S G̲ M̍ P N Ṡ |
| (iv) | *Avaroh* | Ṡ N D̲ P M̍ G̲ R̲ S |
| (v) | *Vādī* | P |

| | | |
|---|---|---|
| (vi) | *Saṁvādī* | S |
| (vii) | *Pakaḍ* | Ṇ S, M̍ G̲, P G̲, R̲ S |
| (viii) | Singing time | 4 p.m. to 7 p.m. |

## *Svar-vistār*

(a) Ṇ, S, M̍ G̲, M̍ P, D̲ P, N, Ṡ, Ṡ N D̲ P, M̍, G̲, P, G̲, R̲ S.

(b) P G̲, R̲, S, Ṇ, S, M̍ G̲, P, M̍ P, D̲ P, M̍ G̲, G̲ M̍ P, G̲, R̲ S, Ṇ, S.

## *Remarks*

1. The slight touch of M̍ prior to G̲ produces a very pleasant effect, such as in N S M̍ G̲ R̲ S; M̍ has been used as the *kaṇ svar* to the main *svar* G̲ (see section 3.9, xxxvi).
2. Singers generally stay for some time on notes S, P, N (rest notes), this gives a pleasant feeling to the listeners. *Tān*s also end generally on these *svar*s.
3. This *rāg* is sung in all the three *saptak*s.
4. In this *rāg*, *ālāp*s and *tān*s generally originate from Ṇ, i.e. *niṣād* of the *mandra̲ saptak.*
5. If R and D (in their *tīvra̲* form) are used — one gets another *rāg* known as *Madhuvantī.*
6. It is a *parmelpraveśak rāg* (see section 3.9, xlii) because after singing this *rāg,* singers can smoothly switch on to the *rāg*s belonging to the *Pūrvī* and *Mārwā thāṭ*s.

### 7.19 Rāg Pahāṛī

| | | |
|---|---|---|
| (i) | Base *thāṭ* | *Bilāwal* |
| (ii) | *Jāti* | *Ouḍav* |
| (iii) | *Āroh* | S R G P D Ṡ |
| (iv) | *Avaroh* | Ṡ D P, G P, G R S |

| | | |
|---|---|---|
| (v) | *Vādī* | S |
| (vi) | *Saṁvādī* | P |
| (vii) | *Pakaḍ* | G, R S, Ḍ, P̣ Ḍ S, G P D P, G, R S Ḍ |
| (viii) | Singing time | Any time during day or night |

*Svar-vistār*

(a) S, R G, G R, S R G R, S R S, Ṇ Ḍ, P̣, Ḍ S R G, G M G R, S R G S, Ṇ Ḍ, G, R S.

(b) S, R G, M G R, S, R G R, S R S Ṇ Ḍ, P̣ Ḍ S, R G R S.

*Remarks*

1. In this *rāg* normally M and N are forbidden in the *āroh* and scarcely used in *avaroh*. This fact makes this *rāg* quite similar to the *rāg Bhūpālī*. Hence, M and N are used little more so as to differentiate it from *Bhūpālī*. As such, it is not possible to exactly describe the *jāti* of the *Pahāṛī rāg*.
2. This *rāg* is mainly used for the composition of *bhajans*, *ṭhumrīs*, *ghazals*, etc. To make these compositions melodious, notes of other *rāgs* are also mixed into *Pahāṛī*.
3. It can be called a *saṅkīrṇa̱ rāg*. By mixing other *rāgs* it gives rise to extremely melodious *ṭhumrīs* and *ghazals*.
4. It is mainly sung in the *mandra̱* and *madhya̱ saptaks*.
5. It can be sung at any time during the day or night.

**7.20 Rāg Pīlū**

| | | |
|---|---|---|
| (i) | Base *thāṭ* | *Kāfī* |
| (ii) | *Jāti* | *Sampūrṇa̱ – Sampūrṇa̱* |
| (iii) | *Āroh* | Ṇ S, G̱ R G̱, M P, Ḏ P, Ṉ D P, Ṡ |
| (iv) | *Avaroh* | Ṡ Ṉ D P M G̱, Ṇ S |
| (v) | *Vādī* | G̱ |

| | | |
|---|---|---|
| (vi) | *Saṁvādī* | N |
| (vii) | *Pakaḍ* | Ṇ S, G̲, Ṇ S, P̣ Ḍ̲, Ṇ S |
| (viii) | Singing time | 1 to 4 p.m. |

### *Svar-vistār*

(a) Ṇ S G̲, Ṇ S, Ṇ, S G̲ R S, Ṇ Ḍ̲, P̣, P̣ P̣ Ḍ̲ Ṇ̲ S, G̲, Ṇ̲ S.

(b) Ṇ S G̲, M G̲, P G̲, D̲, P, M P G̲, Ṇ S G̲, R, S, S R̲ Ṇ, Ḍ̲ P̣, Ṃ P̣ Ḍ̲ Ṇ Ḍ̲ Ṇ S, G̲, R̲, S

### *Remarks*

1. *Pīlū* is a very popular and melodious *rāg* which is quite often used for composing *ṭhumrīs*, *ṭappās*, *dādrās* and *bhajans*.
2. It is a *Saṅkīrṇa̲ rāg* (see section 2.13.2 — point 3). Hence singers mix other *rāgs* also while singing a composition in *rāg Pīlū*. *Miśra̲* (mixed with other *rāgs*) *Pīlū* sounds still sweeter. Efficient singers make use of all the twelve *svars* to enhance the melody. As such this *rāg* may be regarded as a *Sampūrṇa̲-Sampūrṇa̲ rāg*. After giving the shadow of some other *rāgs*, singers return to *Pīlū* by using the note-combination G̲ Ṇ S. The *rāgs* which are generally mixed may be *Bhairavī*, *Bhīmpalāsī*, *Paṭdīp*, etc.
3. This *rāg* is mostly sung in *mandra̲* and *madhya̲ saptaks*.
4. Compositions in *Pīlū* are frequently sung during *Holī* festival in India.

## 7.21 Rāg Pūriādhanāśrī

| | | |
|---|---|---|
| (i) | Base *thāṭ* | *Pūrvī* |
| (ii) | *Jāti* | *Sampūrṇa̲–Sampūrṇa̲* |
| (iii) | *Āroh* | Ṇ R̲ G M̍ P, D̲ P, N Ṡ |
| (iv) | *Avaroh* | Ṙ̲ N D̲ P, M̍ G, M̍ R̲ G, R̲ S |

| | | |
|---|---|---|
| (v) | *Vadī* | P |
| (vi) | *Saṁvadī* | R̲ |
| (vii) | *Pakaḍ* | Ṇ R̲ G, M̍P, D̲ P, M̍G, M̍R̲ G, D̲, M̍G, R̲ S. |
| (viii) | Singing time | Evening 4 p.m. to 7 p.m. |

## *Svar-vistār*

(a) G, R̲ S, Ṇ R̲ S, G, R̲ G, P, M̍ D̲, P, M̍G, M̍ R̲ G, M̍ D̲ M̍G, G, R̲ S.

(b) M̍ G R̲ S, D̲ M̍ G R̲ S, Ṇ R̲ G P, M̍G, M̍ R̲ G R̲ S, N D̲ P D̲ P, D̲ M̍ G, R̲ G, P, M̍ G, M̍ G R̲ S, Ṇ R̲, S.

(c) Ṇ S, G M̍ P, M̍ P, D̲ P, N D̲, P, Ṙ̲ N D̲, P, M̍ P, M̍ G, M̍R̲ G, M̍ D̲ M̍ G, G, R̲ S.

## *Remarks*

1. This *rāg* differs from the *rāg Pūrvī* because the latter uses both the varieties of *madhyam* whereas in the *rāg Pūriādhanāśrī* only *tīvra̲ madhyam* is used.

## 7.22 Rāg Rāgeśwarī

| | | |
|---|---|---|
| (i) | Base *thāṭ* | *Khamāj* |
| (ii) | *Jāti* | *Ouḍav-Ṣāḍav* |
| (iii) | *Āroh* | S G M D N̲ Ṡ |
| (iv) | *Avaroh* | Ṡ N̲ D M G R S |
| (v) | *Vādī* | G |
| (vi) | *Saṁvādī* | N̲ |
| (vii) | *Pakaḍ* | G M D N̲ D, M G R, S. |
| (viii) | Singing time | Night 10 p.m.–1 a.m. |

## *Svar-vistār*

(a) S, R S N̲̣ Ḍ, N̲̣ S, M, M G, M D M G, M G R S, G M.

(b) G M, D M, D N̲ D M, G M D, Ṡ N̲ D, N̲ D M, G M R S.

(c) M G M D, N̲ Ṡ, N̲ D, Ṙ Ṡ N̲ D, M, D G, D N̲ D M, G R S.

*Remarks*

1. The note-combination D M sounds very pleasant.
2. Some singers use both the varieties of *niṣād*.

## 7.23 Rāg Śuddh Kalyāṇ

| (i) | Base *thāṭ* | *Kalyāṇ* |
|---|---|---|
| (ii) | *Jāti* | *Ouḍav–Sampūrṇa* |
| (iii) | *Āroh* | S R G P D Ṡ |
| (iv) | *Avaroh* | Ṡ N D P M̍ G R S |
| (v) | *Vādī* | G |
| (vi) | *Saṁvādī* | D |
| (vii) | *Pakaḍ* | G, R S, Ṇ Ḍ P̣, S, G R, P R, S. |
| (viii) | Singing time | First part of night: 7 to 10 p.m. |

*Svar-vistār*

(a) G, R, S, G, $^{G}$P͡G, $^{G}$D P G, R, G, R, S R S.

(b) P̣, Ḍ P̣, Ṇ Ḍ, P̣, S Ṇ Ḍ P̣, S, R S, G, P̣͡P G, P, R, S R S.

(c) S, R S, G R S, P̣ Ḍ P̣ S, G̣ P̣ Ḍ P̣, S, R S, G R S, G P G R S, D P G R S, N D, P, G P G R S.

***Note***: In (a), $^{G}$P͡G means one has to go from the *svar* P to G by *mīṇḍ;* (see section 3, xxxiv), and G at the top of P means G is the *kaṇ svar* of P (see section 3, xxxvi).

*Remarks*

1. The *āroh* of this *rāg* is similar to that of the *rāg Bhūpālī,* while the *avaroh* is similar to that of the *rāg Yaman.* Hence, some musicologists prefer to call it *Bhūp-Kalyāṇ.*

2. It is to be noted that in *Bhūpālī*, M and N are totally forbidden, but in *Śuddh-Kalyāṇ* these are used in the *avaroh*.

## 7.24 Rāg Tilak-Kāmod

| | | |
|---|---|---|
| (i) | Base *thāṭ* | *Khamāj* |
| (ii) | *Jāti* | *Ṣāḍav–Sampūrṇa* |
| (iii) | *Āroh* | S R G S, R M P D M P, Ṡ. |
| (iv) | *Avaroh* | Ṡ P D M G, S R G, S, Ṇ. |
| (v) | *Vādī* | R |
| (vi) | *Saṁvādī* | P |
| (vii) | *Pakaḍ* | P̣ Ṇ S R G, S, R P M G, S Ṇ. |
| (viii) | Singing time | 10 p.m. to 1 a.m. |

### *Svar-vistār*

(a) P̣ṆSRG, S, R, P, MG, S, RG, S, Ṇ, P̣ṆSRG, S.

(b) S, ṆS, P̣ṆS, RGS, GRPMG, S, RG, S, Ṇ, S, PD, MG, SRG, S, Ṇ, P̣ṆSRG, S.

(c) S, ṆS, G, S, PMG, SDMG, S, Ṡ, PD, MG, S, ṠṘṠ, P, DMG, S, Ṇ, P̣ṆSRGS.

### *Remarks*

1. It is said that this *rāg* has folk origin; perhaps this is the reason that many *svar*s of this *rāg* are used in *vakra* manner.
2. Generally singers use both the *niṣād*s in the *rāg*, however there are few who do not use N̲.
3. According to some musicologists, the *vādī* of this *rāg* is *ṛṣabh* while some others regard *ṣaḍja* as the *vādī svar*.

### 7.25 Rāg Yaman

| | | |
|---|---|---|
| (i) | Base *thāṭ* | *Kalyāṇ* |
| (ii) | *Jāti* | *Sampūrṇa–Sampūrṇa* |
| (iii) | *Āroh* | S R G M̍ P D N Ṡ |
| (iv) | *Avaroh* | Ṡ N D P M̍ G R S |
| (v) | *Vādī* | G |
| (vi) | *Saṁvādī* | N |
| (vii) | *Pakaḍ* | Ṇ R G R, S, P M̍ G, R, S. |
| (viii) | Singing time | First part of night: 7 p.m. to 10 p.m. |

*Svar-vistār*

(a) G, R, S, Ṇ R, S, Ṇ, R G, R G, M̍ G, P, M̍ G, R G, R, Ṇ, R, S.

(b) Ṇ R G, R S, S, Ṇ Ḍ, Ṇ Ḍ, P̣, P̣ Ḍ Ṇ, Ḍ Ṇ, R, G R, Ṇ R G, R, Ṇ R, S.

(c) S, R G, P, M̍, G, R, G M̍ P D N D P M̍, D P M̍ G, P M̍ G, R, P, R, S.

*Remarks*

1. In older texts P is forbidden in *Yaman* but now P is freely used making the *rāg Sampūrṇa*.
2. If M is used even scarcely then we get another variety of *Yaman* known as *Yaman-Kalyāṇ*.

### 7.26 The Importance of Svar-Vistār

In the description of *rāgs* given in sections 7.1 to 7.25, two or three examples of *svar vistār* have been given for each *rāg*. In these patterns of notes or *svars*, the position of comma is important as it indicates where to take a pause. Apart from the examples of *svar-vistār* mentioned, several others can be framed by a proper synthesis of various groups of notes which sound pleasant and belong to the *rāg* under consideration. Such note-combinations should be tried in different *saptak*s and in double speed (*duguṇ-laya̲*) also. This helps in elaborating and extending the *rāg*, thereby making it richer and rhythmic.

Another point to be remembered about the *svar-vistār* is that despite the use of all possible notation symbols (the symbols generally used are those suggested by Pandit Bhatkhande), it is impossible to completely describe the *gāyakī* (singing process) of a singer. Although there are symbols for depicting various singing actions, during the actual singing process so many musical operations are performed that putting them in the notation form can make the presentation more complicated and confusing rather than informative and useful. Hence, in order to learn the intricacies of the art of singing, a suitable teacher is a must. The *svar-vistār* only helps in understanding the basic structure or framework of a *rāg*. This has to be ornamented with *tān*s in different *laya̲* and *saptak*s and the delicate use of such singing techniques as *kaṇ, khaṭkā, murkī, gamak, mīṇḍ*, etc., which can never be completely described on paper.

## 7.27 Modification of Rāgs

[Some musicians believe that certain *rāg*s of Hindustani classical music originated from folk music. Different types of songs are sung on different occasions. Some songs were sad, some expressed joy whereas some were devoted to *bhakti*. These tunes which came out spontaneously from the hearts of the singers had pleasing and soothing effect. Later, musicologists identified various note-combinations in the folk songs and developed them into various *rāg*s. These *rāg*s were then given theoretical basis. Rules for their singing were framed and recorded so that these could be preserved.]

The *khayāl gāyakī* was introduced into the Hindustani classical music in the sixteenth century. This was the period when *dhrupad* style of singing was prevalent which had very little flexibility. The purpose of inducting the *khayāl* singing was to increase the melodic quality and thus enhance the entertainment level. It is quite obvious that if the same sentence is uttered by two persons in different styles and moods, the resultant impact on the listeners will be vastly different. The same is true about the singing process. Two singers may sing the same *rāg*, but if they pause at different places, emphasise on different notes or make use of a particular note-combination more often, then the same *rāg* would produce somewhat different effect although both are using the same notes as required by the *rāg* being sung.

It is important to note that the Hindi word *rāg* means "joy." Hence, it is absolutely essential that the rendering of a *rāg* should create a wave of joy in the hearts of the listeners. While describing the characteristics of a *rāg*, the musical texts put the greatest emphasis on the melodious effect that the *rāg* must produce. The other requirements of a *rāg*, i.e. the base-*thāṭ*, *jāti*, *vādī*, *saṁvādī*, etc. are just the means to keep the musical composition within the framework of a *rāg*. If a singer follows all the rules prescribed for singing a *rāg* but fails to awaken the emotion of joy, his singing would not be meaningful however religiously he might have followed the grammar of the *rāg*.

It has been observed in many cases that the presentation of the same *rāg* by different artists have different "appeal." This is due to the fact that some innovative singers do not merely stick to the prescribed instructions for singing a *rāg* but make a few changes here and there. Sometimes these changes enhance the melodic level of the *rāg*. For example, certain singers use some other *svar* as *vādī* or *saṁvādī* than those given in the musical texts. Some musicians make beautiful use of *vivādī svar* (forbidden note) rather frequently. Some singers work out a different note-combination (other than those normally used) from the *svar*s prescribed for a *rāg*, which gives a new colour to their presentation. But one point should be clear that such changes are not made simply for the sake of creating a variety. A few devoted and highly talented musicians during their intense *riāẓ* (practice) spontaneously come out with such modifications. Thus they start singing a particular *rāg* in their own characteristic style. Normally such imaginative and melodious singers create their own school or *gharānā* of music.

Even the musicologists respect their views on the *chalan* (pattern or way of singing) of a *rāg*.

Sometimes modification of a *rāg* is so significant that it gives rise to a new *rāg*, which can be differentiated from the original *rāg*. For example, the famous musician Tānsen developed many new varieties of certain *rāg*s such as *Miyāṅ kī Toḍī, Miyāṅ kī Sāraṅg, Miyāṅ Malhār,* etc. The creation of new *rāg*s is an ongoing process. Here it can be mentioned that a few years back, the famous *sitār* maestro Pandit Ravi Shankar created many new *rāg*s such as *rāg Parmeśvarī, Jogeśvarī, Tilak śyām* etc. Likewise, the great *sarod* artist Ustad Ali Akbar Khan developed a new *rāg* known as *Chandranandan.*

# Glossary

***abhaṅg***: *bhajan*s are known as *abhaṅg*s in Maharashtra state of western India.

***achal***: fixed, immovable.

***ākār***: (singing) without using words of the song or *sargam*.

***alaṁkār* (also known as *palṭā*)**: combination of musical notes in different sequences (see sections 2.12 and 3.9, xxxix).

***ālāp***: style of singing in slow tempo that involves exposition and elaboration of a *rāg* (sections 3.3 and 3.4.1).

***alpatva̱***: scarcely used (section 3.9, xl).

***anibaddh***: style of singing not bound by rhythm (section 3.3).

***aniṣṭatā***: dissonance, unpleasantness (section 2.6.1).

***antarā***: the latter portion of a song or *bandiś* (section 3.4).

***anudātt***: a note of comparatively lower frequency (sections 1.3 and 2.5).

***anuvād***: pleasant combination of notes; normal *iṣṭatā* (section 2.6.1).

***anuvādī***: notes used in a *rāg* other than *vādī* and *saṁvādī* (section 2.13).

***āroh***: notes in ascending order (sections 2.9 and 3.9, viii).

***āśraya̱ rāg***: dependent *rāg* (section 2.10).

***aṣṭak***: a group of 8 notes, octave (section 2.10.1).

***aṭhguṇ laya̱***: when tempo is eight times the original tempo (section 2.17).

***ati-drut laya̱***: very fast tempo (section 2.15.3).

***ati-mandra̱ saptak***: a *saptak* containing 7 notes having frequencies lower than those in the *mandra̱ saptak* (section 2.7.1).

***ati-tār saptak***: a *saptak* containing 7 notes of frequencies higher than those in the *tār saptak.*

***ati-vilambit laya̱***: very slow tempo (section 2.15.3).

***avanaddh vādya̱***: percussion instrument.

***avaroh***: notes in descending order (sections 2.9 and 3.9, viii).

***āvartan***: cycle, time required for completing one cycle of a *tāl* (section 2.15.1).

***āvirbhāv***: emergence (section 3.9 xli).

***baḍā khayāl***: a style of singing in very slow tempo (section 3.4.1).

***bahutva̱***: frequently used (section 3.9, xl).

***bandiś***: a musical composition (section 3.4).

***bhajan***: a devotional song (section 3.6).

***bhakti***: devotion to God (section 1.11).

***bhāv***: mood (section 2.6.1).

***bol***: words of a *bandiś* or song; different types of sound produced from *tablā* or *sitār* (sections 2.15.1 and 3.9, xxi).

***bol-ālāp***: singing in a slow tempo using the words of the song (sections 3.4.1 and 3.9, xxiv).

***bol-tān***: singing in a faster tempo using the words of the song (sections 3.4.1 and 3.9, xxxiii).

***boul-saṅgīt*:** devotional music of Bengal state in eastern India (section 3.7.6).

***chaitī*:** a variety of folk music popular in the northern part of India (Uttar Pradesh).

***chalan*:** the way notes are used while rendering a *rāg;* pattern.

***chauguṇ*:** four time (the speed or *laya̲* of singing).

***Chhāyā-lag rāg*:** more or less similar *rāg* (section 2.13.2).

***chhoṭā khayāl*:** style of singing a *bandiś* at a faster tempo than that of the *baḍā-khayāl* (section 3.4.2).

***dādrā*:** a particular type of singing of semi-classical music set to *dādrā tāl* (section 3.5.5).

***deśī saṅgīt*:** music which is totally entertainment-oriented (section 3.1).

***dhaivat*:** the 6th note of the Indian musical scale.

***dhamār* and *dhrupad*:** an old style of singing that existed prior to *khayāl* singing.

***dhun*:** tune of a musical composition.

***dhvani*:** sound.

***d̲rut laya̲*:** fast tempo (section 2.15.3).

***duguṇ laya̲*:** double (speed of singing).

***gamak*:** an operation used during singing (section 3.9, xxxv).

***gāndhār*:** the third note of the musical scale (section 2.7).

***gāyakī*:** style of singing .

***gāyan*:** process of singing.

***garbā*:** devotional song popular in Gujarat state in western India.

***gat*:** composition played on a musical instrument.

***gaẓ*:** bow for playing a stringed instrument.

***ghazal***: a popular variety of singing light music using Urdu poetry.

***gīt***: a song or a lyrical poetry.

***ghan-vādya***: musical instrument in which sound is produced by striking a metal or some other material.

***gharānā***: tradition or school (of music).

***ghoḍī***: a variety of folk music.

***guru***: teacher.

***holī***: a variety of folk music; a Hindu festival.

***iṣṭatā***: consonance, pleasant combination of notes (section 2.6.1).

***jāti***: class of *rāgs* (section 2.13.1).

***jugalbandī***: a programme in which two singers or instrumentalists perform together.

***kajarī***: a variety of folk music.

***kaṇ***: an operation during singing (section 3.9, xxxvi).

**Karnatic music:** music system of south India.

***kawwālī***: a variety of semi-classical music (section 3.5.4).

***kawwāl***: artist who sings *kawwālī*.

***kīrtan***: devotional music.

***khālī***: a particular time position indicated by the symbol written below the *bol* of a *tāl*.

***khaṇḍ* or *vibhāg***: part or section of a *tāl* (section 2.16).

***khaṭkā***: an operation during singing (section 3.9, xxxviii).

***khayāl***: a musical composition sung in a particular style.

***komal***: variety of a note, flat note.

***lakṣaṇ-gīt***: a song composed in such a way that it represents all the characteristics of a *rāg*.

***lāvaṇī***: a variety of folk music of Maharashtra state of India.

***laya̲***: tempo (of singing).

***madhya̲ laya̲***: neither fast nor low tempo.

***madhya̲ saptak***: central *saptak* in between *mandra̲* and *tār saptak*.

***madhyam***: 4th note of the musical scale.

***mandra̲ saptak***: musical scale in which notes have lower frequencies (see Table 2.3).

***mārgī-saṅgīt***: celestial music, ancient devotional music.

***mātrā***: time-interval between two beats of a *tāl* (section 2.15.2).

***mīṇḍ***: an operation during singing (section 3.9, xxxiv).

***miśra rāg***: a *rāg* in which other *rāg*s have been mixed.

***mizrāb***: plectrum of wire or some other device to strike the strings of a musical instrument.

***mūrchhanā***: mathematical arrangement of notes according to a particular scheme.

***mukhaḍā***: the first line of a *bandiś* or song.

***murkī***: an operation during singing process (section 3.9, xxxvii).

***nād***: sound of a particular frequency.

***nāṭya̲-saṅgīt***: music used during the performance of drama.

***nibaddh-gāyan***: a composition sung with rhythm (section 3.4).

***niṣād***: the 7th note of the musical scale.

***nṛtya̲***: dance.

***nyās***: the note at which a singer can stay for some time; rest note.

***ouḍav-rāg***: a class of *rāg* which uses only five notes (section 2.13.1).

***palṭā***: various patterns of notes or *bols* played on the *tablā* or *sitār* (section 2.12). see *alaṁkār*.

***pañcham***: the 5th note of the musical scale.

***paṇḍit***: expert in a particular subject.

***pūrvāṅgvādī rāg***: a class of *rāgs* (section 2.14).

***rāg***: a characteristic combination of notes which gives rise to various musical compositions of similar mood.

***riāẓ***: practice.

***r̥ṣabh***: 2nd note of the musical scale.

***sam***: starting point of a *tāl* (section 2.15.4).

***Sampūrṇa̲ rāg***: a class of *rāgs* which uses seven notes of the musical scale.

***sampradāya̲***: a school representing and following a particular style.

***saṁvādī***: 2nd prominent note of a *rāg*.

***Sāmaveda̲***: a religious treatise of Hindus.

***Sandhi-prakāś rāg***: *rāg* sung during sunrise and sunset.

***Saṅkīrṇa̲ rāg***: *rāg* created by mixing two or more *rāgs*.

***saṅgīt***: music.

***saptak***: serial arrangement of the seven notes of the musical scale.

***sargam***: utterance of the names of various notes such as S, R, G, M, etc. during singing.

***ṣaḍja̲***: the 1st note of the musical scale.

***ṣaḍja̲ madhyam bhāv***: pleasant combination of the 1st and 4th notes of the musical scale (section 2.6.1).

***ṣaḍja̲-pañcham bhāv***: pleasant combination of the 1st and the 5th notes of the musical scale (section 2.6.1).

***ṣāḍav rāg***: *rāg* containing only six notes of the musical scale (section 2.13.1).

***śāstra*:** treatise.

***śiṣya*:** student.

***ślok*:** description in the form of couplets of Sanskrit poetry.

***śruti*:** see section 2.5.

***śuddh rāg*:** see section 2.13.2.

***sohar*:** a variety of folk songs.

***sūfī*:** a Muslim saint.

***sūt*:** an operation while playing stringed instruments.

***sthāyī*:** the first part of a song which is repeatedly sung at various intervals during the singing process; also called *mukhaḍā* (section 3.4).

***suṣir vādya*:** musical instruments in which wind is to be blown in, to produce sound (section 6.4).

***svar*:** *nād* or musical note of a particular frequency (section 2.5 and Table 2.1).

***svarit*:** *svar* whose frequency is neither high nor low.

***svarūp*:** picture or mood (of a *rāg*).

***tāl*:** a particular pattern of *bol*s (beats) in a percussion instrument like *tablā* (sections 2.15.1 and 2.16).

***tālī*:** clap during *tablā* playing to emphasise certain *bol*s.

***tān*:** a sequence of various notes uttered rather rapidly during singing.

***ṭappā*:** a typical style of singing originated from northern India.

***tarab*:** sympathetic strings which resonate when the main strings of a stringed instrument are plucked by a plectrum (section 6.9.1).

***tarānā*:** a variety of singing in very fast tempo (section 3.4.3).

***tār-saptak*:** *saptak* in which frequencies of notes are higher than those in the *madhya saptak* (Table 2.3).

***tat-vādya̲***: a stringed instrument.

***tīvra̲***: a variety of a note, sharp note.

***thāṭ***: a particular group of seven notes from which many *rāg*s can be derived (section 2.10).

***ṭhekā***: one cycle of the basic rhythm (*tāl*) in a percussion instrument like *tablā*.

***ṭhumrī***: a variety of singing in semi-classical music (section 3.5.2).

***tirobhāv***: deviation from the notes of the *rāg* being sung for short period, in order to conceal the *rāg* for a while.

***uddātt***: a note of relatively higher frequency.

***up-jāti***: sub-class (section 2.13.1).

***ustād***: an expert, teacher.

***uttarāṅg-vādī rāg***: a class of *rāg*s (section 2.14).

***vādan***: playing musical instrument.

***vādī svar***: the most prominent and very frequently used note in a *rāg*.

***vādya̲***: a musical instrument.

***vakra̲***: use of a note in an indirect manner (section 3.9, xxxi).

***varjit svar***: forbidden note in a *rāg*.

***varṇa̲s***: different styles of using the notes while singing (section 2.11).

***vikr̥t***: a variety of note (Table 2.4).

***vistār***: expansion, elaboration.

***vitat-vādya̲***: a string instrument played with a bow.

***vivād***: unpleasant note-combination (section 2.6.1).

***vivādī***: the forbidden note in a *rāg*.

# Bibliography


Bandyopadhyaya, S., *The Origin of Rāg*, New Delhi: Munshiram Manoharlal Publishers.

Bhatkhande, Vishnu Narayan, *Kramik Pustak Mālikā*, vols. 1 to 6, Hathras, UP: Sangeet Karyalaya, 2008.

Brahaspati, Acharya, *Saṅgīt Chintāmaṇi*, Hathras, UP: Sangeet Karyalaya, 1989.

Brahaspati, Kailash Chandradev, *Bharat kā Saṅgīt Siddhānt*, Lucknow, UP: Uttar Pradesh Hindi Sansthan, 1991.

Durga, S.A.K., *Voice Culture*, Baroda, Gujarat: The Indian Musicological Society, 2003.

Jha, Pandit Ramashraya, *Abhinav Gītāñjali*, vols. 1 to 5, Allahabad, UP: Sangeet Sadan Prakashan, 2009.

Joshi, Umesh, *Bhartīya̱ Saṅgīt kā Itihās*, Agra, UP: Mansarovar Prakashan.

Mishra, Shrirajeshwar, *Saṅgīt Ratnākar*, New Delhi: Radhakrishna Prakashan, 1999.

Mukherji, Kumar Prasad, *The Lost World of Hindustani Music*, New Delhi: Penguin Books, 2006.

Nadkarni, Mohan, *The Great Masters: Profiles in Hindustani Classical Vocal Music*, New Delhi: Rupa & Co., 2005.

Neuman, Daniel M., *The Life of Music in North India*, London (UK): The University of Chicago Press Ltd., 1980.

Sharma, Bhagwat Sharan, *Bhārtīya̱ Sangeet kā Itihās*, Hathras, UP: Sangeet Karyalaya, 1993.

Singh, Lalit Kishore, *Dhvani aur Saṅgīt*, New Delhi: Bhartiya Jnanpeeth, 2004.

Vasant, *Saṅgīt Viśārad*, Hathras, UP: Sangeet Karyalaya, 2007.

# Name Index

# Book Index

# Tāl Index

# Rāg Index

# Subject Index




(see book index also on page 175)